A KILLER ON CAMPUS

RHONDA STARNES

LOVE INSPIRED SUSPENSE
INSPIRATIONAL ROMANCE

LOVE INSPIRED® SUSPENSE
INSPIRATIONAL ROMANCE

Recycling programs for this product may not exist in your area.

ISBN-13: 978-1-335-90681-6

A Killer on Campus

Love Inspired
22 Adelaide St. West, 41st Floor
Toronto, Ontario M5H 4E3, Canada
www.LoveInspired.com

HarperCollins Publishers
Macken House, 39/40 Mayor Street Upper,
Dublin 1, D01 C9W8, Ireland
www.HarperCollins.com

Printed in U.S.A.

1 2 3 4 5 6 7 8 9 10 HDC 28 27 26 25

Beep, beep, beep! The shrills of the smoke alarm sounded in the hall, followed by people yelling and running. Jane grasped the door handle with her free hand and tugged. It didn't budge.

I'm locked in! Panic welled inside her. There were no windows in the room. How was she going to get out?

She pounded on the steel door with the sides of her fists. "Help! I'm locked inside! Someone, please, help!"

Nausea grew in her and a feeling of faintness enveloped her.

The door lurched beneath her hands.

"Jane!" Ridge yelled. "Are you in there?"

"Ridge," she cried. "I'm locked in." Tears burned the backs of her eyes. *Please let him get me out.*

"I have to get help. I'll be right back."

"Hurry." Jane pressed her cheek against the cool metal door. "There's gas or something coming through the vents."

Silence followed. Had he heard her plea before he went for help? She glanced around. A dense haze filled the small room. She mumbled to herself, "Ridge *will* get it open. He won't leave me trapped in here."

Please, hurry. Before I die.

Rhonda Starnes is a retired middle-school language arts teacher who dreamed of being a published author from the time she was in seventh grade and wrote her first short story. She lives in North Alabama with her husband, whom she lovingly refers to as Mountain Man. They enjoy traveling and spending time with their children and grandchildren. Rhonda writes heart-and-soul suspense with rugged heroes and feisty heroines.

Books by Rhonda Starnes

Love Inspired Suspense

Rocky Mountain Revenge
Perilous Wilderness Escape
Tracked Through the Mountains
Abducted at Christmas
Uncovering Colorado Secrets
Cold Case Mountain Murder
Smoky Mountain Escape
In a Killer's Crosshairs
Ambushed in the Night
A Killer on Campus

Visit the Author Profile page at LoveInspired.com.

Let all bitterness, and wrath, and anger, and
clamour, and evil speaking, be put away from you,
with all malice: And be ye kind one to another,
tenderhearted, forgiving one another,
even as God for Christ's sake hath forgiven you.
—*Ephesians* 4:31–32

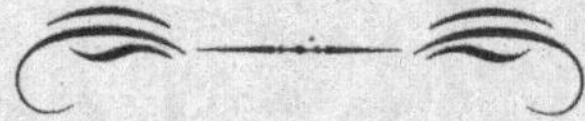

For Kristy, Clyde and Quintin.
I would not have finished this book without you.
Love y'all!

ONE

Adjunct professor Jane Mason glanced out the window of her second-floor classroom. An inky black sky with a smattering of stars and no moon blanketed the Blackberry Falls Community College campus. The large round clock on the back wall showed it was already 10:45 p.m. Where had the time gone? She hadn't intended to stay on campus this late.

It was finals week for the summer semester, so her Foundations of Forensic Photography students could leave class as they submitted their exams. Her last student had left almost two hours ago, but Jane had remained to grade the exams, feeling the need to wrap up her duties as quickly as possible so she could focus on solving her Aunt Nikki's murder before Grandma Mason's dementia stole the rest of her memories.

Jane had never considered her ability to help solve cold cases using photo-enhancing software until Chief Evan Bradshaw approached her with a case involving a hitchhiker killed in a hit-and-run ten years ago—long before she joined the force as a forensic photographer. The officer who'd taken the photos of the crime scene—an untrained photographer—had done the best he could. But rain and fog had made the images useless.

It had taken many hours bent over her laptop, but Jane had successfully cleared up the photos, revealing a partial license plate number the victim had written in the dirt. As a result, the police had arrested a suspect in a matter of weeks.

Local news outlets had flocked to the story. It wasn't until one reporter mentioned Jane's family connection to the Brush Hollow Reservoir Murders—a cold case that had haunted the residents of Blackberry Falls for twenty-three years—that she'd even entertained the thought of solving Aunt Nikki's murder. Now, Jane was worse than a child asking why a thousand times a day. Every free moment she had, she was searching through the archives in the college library and asking questions to the staff members who'd worked on campus when Aunt Nikki had been a student.

She'd heard the story of the murders her entire life. A man and his young son on a fishing trip found the bodies of nineteen-year-old second-year students Nikki and her roommate Phoebe, five days after they disappeared. The evidence indicated that someone had strangled both victims. Police suspected someone murdered them elsewhere and then transported their bodies to the remote location for disposal. There were no signs of forced entry or a struggle in their apartment, and the murder location remained a mystery to this day.

Grandma Mason had lived with the senseless death of her only daughter for nearly a quarter of a century. She deserved closure, even if it would only be a fleeting moment of understanding because of Alzheimer's. Jane would not step away from this case.

While she had always viewed her photography skills as a tool to provide investigators the ability to see minute details perpetrators hoped would remain hidden, helping Evan solve a cold case had given her even greater satisfaction. Using photo-editing software to enhance blurry or overexposed pictures and sharpening the image so every detail was clear had felt like pulling back a curtain to reveal a surprise. Thankfully, the results of her efforts had produced the desired outcome and the hit-and-run murderer was behind bars. It would happen again. This time for Aunt Nikki and Phoebe. Jane would make sure of it.

A shudder danced along Jane's spine, and her entire body shook. For the first time, she noticed the eerie blanket of quietness that had settled over the classroom. The ticking clock beat to the rhythm of her heart.

All the evening classes would have been dismissed by now. Even the library would be closed. The librarian, Mrs. Forrester, was a stickler for keeping to the schedule, having students make their way to the door five minutes before closing. Mrs. Forrester would have filed out behind them, turning off the lights and locking the door at ten o'clock on the dot. Jane doubted she'd see another soul on her way out, since the parking lot would probably also be empty.

Time to go home. She would come in early tomorrow and finish up before her Photography 101 class. The students were presenting their portfolios, which would count for 30 percent of their final grade, and completing a short final exam. Thankfully, her teaching assistant would be around to help grade the portfolios and enter the final grades into the computer. Which would allow Jane time to finish the end-of-semester paperwork, setting her free to work on her aunt's case for two weeks before she had to prepare for the fall semester classes to begin.

Turning off her computer, she slid it into her

satchel. Then she stood and draped the strap over her head and across her body. Quickly crossing to the door, she stepped into the hall— lit only by the emergency exit signs and the eerie glow coming from the vending machines at the opposite end. Another shiver raced up her spine.

A bunny hopped over your grave. Granny Mason's raspy voice echoed in the back of Jane's mind.

"That's just an old wives' tale, Granny," she mumbled under her breath.

Her dad's response to seven-year-old Jane crying over one of her great-grandmother's many superstitions came to mind. *Never give in to fear, baby girl. If fear controls you, you'll never be free.*

Straightening her shoulders and releasing a slow breath, she pulled her keys out of the front pocket of her satchel. Then promptly dropped them on the floor. What was wrong with her? Why was she so jittery tonight? She had never been one to be afraid of shadows in the dark.

Unlike her cousin Carolina, who only watched sappy love stories and cooking shows, Jane spent most of her evenings watching murder mysteries and true crime dramas. Her mind, always intrigued, worked to figure out the clues. That, along with her love of photography, was what led her to earn a master's degree in criminal justice with a focus on crime scene photography.

While at the University of Colorado in Denver, she'd met and fallen in love with Barry, who was a business major. He graduated a semester before her and accepted a job in Chicago. Dreaming of a future with Barry, Jane had planned to move to be closer to him. As her final semester drew to a close, she had been offered her dream job in Chicago.

Two days later, her twin brother, Justin—who had followed their best-friend Ridge Snyder into the Navy straight out of high school—had died in combat. That had been the beginning of the end of hers and Barry's relationship and of Jane's dream of working in a big city.

Her mother's distress at losing her son six months after losing Jane's father to a sudden heart attack—and her fear of losing her only daughter to a job a thousand miles away—had kept Jane home. She'd originally only planned to stay for a few weeks, but Chief Bradshaw had offered her a summer job as a forensic photographer for his office. Then, a month later, an adjunct professor position became available at the college. And in a blink, two months became four years. She enjoyed both jobs, but her work with the Blackberry Falls Police Department wasn't at all what she'd envisioned when she earned her degree. In her four years assisting the police department, she had only photographed one crime scene involving a dead body. In that case, the investigation revealed that the victim hadn't been murdered, but had slipped on ice and fallen on a shovel. The typical crimes in Blackberry Falls, Colorado, population sixteen hundred, mainly comprised robberies, vehicle accidents and high school or college students pulling pranks, like kidnapping their rival's mascot.

Jane straightened and turned to lock her classroom door. She gasped, her hand instinctively covering her mouth to stifle the scream that wanted to escape. Someone had torn out the front-page article the *Blackberry Falls Tribune* had published about her involvement solving the cold case hit-and-run and her desire to find her aunt's killer and taped it to her classroom door. A red marker had been used to draw an image of crosshairs over the photo of her, with her face in the center of the target. Using the same dark red ink, they had written one word below the image… *Bang!*

With a shaky hand, she snatched the paper from the door, whirled and hurried toward the elevator, her footsteps echoing in the long hallway. The sound of a door banging closed came from the opposite end of the hall. She dared a look over her shoulder. A shadowy figure walked toward her with measured steps, the footsteps sounding with a thud. She could not make out his features, but he appeared too tall to be Professor Clinton or Professor Smythe, the only male professors with classrooms on the floor.

She rounded the corner and crossed to the elevator. She raised her finger to press the call button when the sound of the elevator moving caught her attention. Glancing at the floor indicator, she saw the elevator descending from the fifth floor. Who would be on the elevator after-hours? Could it be the janitor? Or did the man behind her have an accomplice? Was that why he hadn't been in a hurry? Had he been leading her into a trap? She wouldn't stick around to find out. Jane darted into the stairwell and began her descent, not even attempting to muffle her footsteps. What was the point? They knew she was there.

Her heart thumped in her chest as she flew down the stairs, thankful that her classroom was on the second floor. As she reached the first-floor landing, she heard the stairwell door to the second floor open. She glanced up. A figure—dressed in black pants and a black hoodie—wearing a white ghost face mask stood on the second-floor landing, staring down at her as the heavy metal door clanged shut behind him.

Fear snaked through her, freezing her in place, her hand on the door handle. She struggled to breathe, her chest tightening as panic overtook her. She met her tormentor's gaze. "Dear Lord, please, help me," she prayed aloud, begging God to spare her, even though she hadn't prayed in four years.

"You should have let the girls rest in peace." The masked man raised his arm, a gun in his hand. Instantly unfrozen, she jerked the door open. A bullet hit the doorframe. She bolted through the doorway. Adrenaline carried her across the foyer as footsteps echoed in the stairwell. Pushing open the entrance door, she glanced over her shoulder. The man stepped out of the stairwell, and Jane raced into the night, maniacal laughter ringing out behind her.

"You can run, but you can't hide," her tormentor yelled tauntingly.

Jane didn't stop running until she reached her MINI Cooper. Her body shaking uncontrollably, she locked herself inside. Then she took a steadying breath and forced herself to focus. Pressing the Start button, she shifted into Drive and pressed down on the gas pedal, tires squealing as she drove toward the exit.

The memory of Aunt Nikki babysitting Jane and playing dress-up flashed through her mind. Anger at the loss of her beautiful aunt tamped down the fear that coursed through her veins. "Aunt Nikki, as Granny Mason would say, I've *stirred up a hornet's nest.*"

Growing up, Jane had had an enormous fear of insects with stingers. Right now, a nest full of hornets was less frightening than the masked man with a gun.

Rolling his shoulders, Ridge Snyder focused on the road ahead of him. It had been an exhausting thirty-six hours. He was ready for a hot shower, food and sleep…and not necessarily in that order. Thankfully, he'd captured Trey Wilborn in Montana before he crossed the Canadian border.

Ridge had never dreamed of becoming a bounty hunter. Yet, here he was, four years after his Navy SEAL career imploded following an ambush that killed his best friend and left Ridge with a left leg full of hardware, chasing down the bad guys. And as much as he enjoyed outsmarting fugitives and earning extra money, being a bounty hunter took a toll on his body. He'd pay the price tomorrow, with achy joints and a pronounced limp.

Harvey Armstrong's orchard came into view.

Ridge rolled down his window, inhaling the sweet scent of peaches as he admired the Milky Way decorating the night sky. A perfect summer's night. His shoulders relaxed. All was right in his world.

The orchard gave way to a field, and the one-story brick house where Jane Mason lived with her cousin Carolina pulled his attention. Sitting a hundred yards off the road, the house, completely dark on the inside, was illuminated by the headlights from Jane's yellow MINI Cooper. Where was she headed this time of night?

"None of your business, buddy," he muttered aloud.

Even though he and Jane had been best friends throughout middle school, high school and well into adulthood, when Justin died, so had their friendship. She blamed him for her twin's death. For years, he'd blamed himself, too. Returning from war injured and without one of his best friends had been difficult. He'd been angry at himself, God and anyone who dared to tell him none of it was his fault, or God's.

When he'd moved home, broken and depressed, his mom had suggested he see a counselor. Actually, she hadn't suggested, she'd insisted. Told him, if he didn't agree to weekly counseling sessions, he couldn't stay on the ranch. And even though she couldn't technically kick him off the ranch, since he was one-third owner of the property, she could have kicked him out of her home, forcing him to sleep in a tent or find other accommodations.

A smile crossed his face as he thought of his mom, all five feet five inches of her coming into his room one afternoon, grabbing his ear and pulling him out of the bed. She'd said there wasn't room on the ranch for anyone who was going to lie around all day and do nothing. Knowing how difficult it must have been for the woman who loved him the most in the world to give him a dose of reality, especially since it meant he'd have to choose to abide by her rules or leave, had been the jolt he'd needed to work through the mental pain. It hadn't been an easy task, but eight months into his twice-weekly counseling sessions, he'd had a breakthrough. Nothing that had happened had been his fault, or God's. Or so he kept trying to convince himself.

Reducing his speed, Ridge craned his neck as he passed Jane's driveway. Why was she just sitting there? Was she going or coming? She'd had plenty of time to get out of the vehicle or pull out of the drive. Something felt off.

He shifted his gaze to the rearview mirror as he continued down the road. She didn't move.

"That's it!" Ridge executed a U-turn. "Something's wrong. Worst-case scenario, she's fine and tells me to leave."

He'd only stopped by once since moving home. That day, Carolina had met him on the front porch and told him Jane didn't want to see him. He'd caught a glimpse of Jane peeking through the curtains, her eyes red and swollen from crying. It had ripped his heart in half. He hadn't attempted to see her since that day. Ridge had never imagined a scenario where Justin and Jane weren't a part of his life.

He activated his blinker, pulled into the driveway and parked his truck behind her compact car. Then he hopped out and jogged over to her as she exited her vehicle, her cell phone pressed to her ear.

"What are you doing here? You scared me." She leaned against the side of her vehicle and spoke into the phone. "No. I'm fine. It's only Ridge… Okay…"

Jane held out her phone. "Evan wants to speak to you."

Ridge furrowed his brow. He'd left Chief Evan Bradshaw fifteen minutes ago, after handing over Trey. Accepting the phone, he lifted it to his ear. "Evan, what's going on?"

"There was an incident at the college when Jane left work this evening."

"What happened?"

"Someone made an attempt on her life. I'm headed to the campus now to meet with the security officer and look at the crime scene."

Crime scene. Ridge tightened his grip on the phone, his eyes scanning Jane for injuries.

"My night duty officer is responding to a single-car accident," Evan continued. "Could you make sure nothing at her house seems amiss and see that she gets inside safely? She's had a pretty harrowing night."

Ridge suspected Jane wouldn't like Evan's idea, but if she were in danger, there was no way Ridge would turn his back and walk away. "Sure. Not a problem." He handed the phone back to her.

She accepted it. "Evan, I'll… There's no need for that… I know… Okay. If you think it's best… Yes, I'll stop by first thing in the morning and file the report… Goodbye."

Jane disconnected the phone and puffed out a breath. "I'm supposed to let you check the house."

Whatever had happened that evening had to be serious for Evan to insist on Ridge filling in when an officer wasn't available. "Carolina isn't home?"

"No. She's in Hawaii with her parents and siblings."

"Why don't you wait in your car?"

"No." She ducked inside her vehicle and emerged with a satchel clutched in her hand. "Evan will expect an *all-clear* text message from you, so I'll allow you to accompany me inside."

Tamping down the desire to argue, he removed his weapon from its shoulder holster. "Okay, but at least allow me to go first. You stay behind me."

She nodded, handed him her key and fell into step behind him. Except for the sound of crickets chirping and a random bullfrog croaking, all was quiet. He tested the door handle. Locked tight. Inserting the key, he opened the door and stepped into the entry area. Five minutes later, he'd checked every room—including all windows and exterior doors—of the small ranch-style home.

Ridge holstered his weapon. "I'll let Evan know the house is undisturbed."

"Thank you."

Silence fell across the room. He had a thousand things he wanted to say, but he doubted she'd want to hear them. *Don't push it, Snyder. Wait for a better time to offer her the apology you've held on to for the past four years.*

He looked around, taking in the decor for the first time. The single-story ranch-style house had a real homey feel to it. A photo gallery, featuring pictures of Jane, Justin and their parents, and Carolina, her siblings and parents, filled one entire wall in the living room. A wave of sadness washed over Ridge. He couldn't help but feel left out, since there were no photos of him on the wall. At one time, he had considered himself Jane and Justin's honorary sibling.

"I appreciate you seeing me inside safely," Jane interrupted his thoughts. "I won't keep you. Evan said you've had a long drive today. I'm sure you're tired."

Ridge had so many questions he wanted answered. What happened at the college? Who attacked Jane? It had to be serious or Evan wouldn't make a trip to the campus in the middle of the night. Pursing his lips, he gave a curt nod. "I'll get out of your way."

He crossed to the door and paused, his hand on the knob. "Do you still have my phone number?"

"What?" She frowned.

"My phone number. Do you still have it listed in your phone?"

"I…" Jane pursed her lips.

Taking out his phone, he quickly sent a message.

Seconds later, her phone dinged.

"There. You have it now. I know that I'm the last person you want to turn to for help." His voice cracked, and he forced himself to swallow past the lump in his throat. "Please, don't let your hatred of me cause you to be reckless. I can reach you faster than the police. If the person who attacked you attempts to break in, calling me first may make the difference in living or dying."

She blanched. He momentarily regretted his words. If he could shield her from the harsh truths of reality, he would, but if her life were in danger, coddling her wouldn't help.

"Good night." Ridge opened the door and stepped outside, pausing in the shadows long enough to hear the deadbolt slide into place before jogging to his truck. He slid into the driver's seat and slumped over the steering wheel, a wave of emotions assailing him.

Nightmares of the ambush in the jungle haunted him most nights. He couldn't do anything to bring Justin back. But he could protect Jane. He raised his head and stared at the house. The living room curtains moved, and Jane peered outside. She was obviously anxious for him to leave.

Starting the vehicle, he shifted into gear, backed down the long drive and turned toward the ranch, certain she was still watching. He drove out of sight, but the thought of her being in her home, alone and vulnerable, gnawed at him. Her closest neighbor lived too far away to hear her yell for help. Would she call Ridge if she were afraid? Or would she rely on the police reaching her in time?

There were no finer men or women in law enforcement than those who worked for the Blackberry Falls Police Department, but being a small town with only one officer working the night shift could mean a slow response. And in an emergency, time was of the essence.

"Lord, how did I get to this point in life? I failed Justin. I can't fail Jane, too."

Executing a U-turn for the second time that evening, he pressed down on the accelerator. An image of Jane's face when she saw him earlier flashed through his mind. He eased off the gas pedal. She would be angry if he returned and insisted on guarding her.

Not if she didn't know he was there. Her house came into view. All the lights were off except for one in the front bedroom. Ridge turned off his headlights and slowed his speed. Pulling off the road and onto the edge of her property, he parked between two pine trees. Turning off the engine, he lowered his windows and reclined his seat. It wouldn't be the restful night he'd hoped for, but he'd slept in much worse conditions. And if Jane needed him, he'd be there.

TWO

Jane flopped onto her right side, bunched her pillow under her neck and glanced at the clock on the nightstand. It was 2:37 a.m. She'd tossed and turned for two hours and hadn't closed her eyes once. Her mind refused to quiet and allow her to sleep. Why had Ridge shown up at her house? She wished she had asked him.

He hadn't stepped foot on the property since Carolina turned him away the day after he moved back home, five months after Justin's funeral. Whatever the reason for his visit, she was glad he'd shown up when he had. Not that she would ever admit it to him. However, once she'd reached her house and the adrenaline had dissipated, the fear of walking into her dark home alone had taken hold. She had hoped Evan could send an officer out to take her statement, and she had planned to wait in the car until they arrived. Which, thinking back on it now, wasn't very smart. If the shooter had followed her home, she would have been an easy target.

Someone tried to kill me. She had never considered not being safe in her small hometown. Murders didn't happen here.

Only they did. The double homicide that had taken her aunt's life twenty-three years ago was proof of that. Aunt Nikki and Phoebe deserved justice. Jane could not let fear take over. She had to find answers.

With a sigh, Jane sat up and swung her legs off the bed. Then she pushed her feet into her slippers and headed down the hall. No use lying in bed, tossing and turning.

Going into the kitchen, she snagged her favorite ceramic mug out of the cabinet and quickly made herself a cup of chai tea using her single-serve coffee maker. She added a splash of cream to the tea and then carried the mug into the bedroom that she had converted into a home office. Not wanting the harsh glare of the overhead light, she switched on the floor lamp and crossed to her desk that sat in front of the only window in the room. Settling into her desk chair, she looked out over the backyard. Illuminated by the full moon, she could make out the shapes of the trees and shrubs and the small garden shed that housed the lawn mower.

The world around her was asleep. A sense of calm enveloped her.

Jane turned her chair to face her desk and pressed the power button on her desktop computer, then she glanced around her office. It was her favorite room in the house. The one place where she could let go of the cares of the world and lose herself in her work and creativity. The world of forensic photography was one of death and violence. To offset the doom and gloom, she made it a priority to take colorful nature photos at every opportunity. Her office reflected this.

Framed prints of her photos of sunsets over the Rocky Mountains decorated pale cream walls. And she had selected room accents to match the colors in the sunsets. A multicolored rug adorned the hardwood floor, and in the corner with a built-in bookcase, she'd placed a sunflower-yellow chair with vibrant pillows and a lightweight cobalt-blue throw blanket. Even though she hadn't opened it in a long time, her favorite Bible sat on the small side table, along with a journal and multicolored pens for note-taking.

While working on her first cold case—the hit-and-run death of a hiker a mile from Temple Canyon trailhead—Jane had discovered being in her home office brought her peace and kept her grounded, keeping her from being engulfed by the pain she had experienced looking at the photo of the crime scene. She could only hope that being in the room would bring her the same peace this time.

She had planned to wrap-up her summer classes before beginning work on her aunt's case, but it wouldn't hurt to get a head start, especially since the killer had made his presence known. Besides, she couldn't sleep. Logging into her official police department email, she located the message Evan had sent with ten photos attached. Evan had included minimal background information for each photo.

The first five photos showed Aunt Nikki's and Phoebe's dead bodies at the reservoir. There were two photos of each girl separately, taken from different angles, and one photo of them together. The sixth photo was of the overall crime scene, and the remaining four photos were of the girls' apartment.

Jane clicked on the sixth photo. The image filled the screen, and she winced. It was so blurry she would have never recognized it as a campsite at Brush Hollow Reservoir if she hadn't already known that to be the case. She imported the photo into her editing software.

A loud eerie, drawn-out fox wail made the hairs on the back of her neck stand at attention. She spun in her chair and peered into the night. Nothing seemed out of place. Another animal must have startled the fox. Possibly a bobcat, which was common in the Colorado countryside.

As she turned back to the room, the glint of a red light to the left of the garden shed caught her attention. It looked like… No, it couldn't be… She dove to the floor seconds before a bullet shattered the window and hit the computer monitor. Rapid fire ensued, bullets peppering the walls and shattering the framed photos.

Her phone was on her nightstand. She had to get to it. Call for help. Staying low, Jane crawled toward the door, getting faster as each gunshot rang out. She was almost to the door when a bullet connected with the glass shade on the floor lamp, casting the room in darkness as shards rained down on her. Jane yelped, pushed to her feet, darted out of the room, down the hall and into her bedroom, thankful it was on the opposite side of the house, putting more walls between her and the shooter.

The instant she crossed the threshold, she gave the command for her phone to call 911.

"Nine-one-one, what's your emergency?"

She snatched her phone off the bedside table and put it to her ear. "This is Jane Mason. I work for the Blackberry Falls Police Department. Someone is outside my home, shooting at me. Please, send help. Fast."

Headlights flashed across her bedroom wall. *No!* Was it the shooter? Had he changed his position, somehow knowing she'd moved rooms? She dropped to the floor, using her bed as a shield.

Don't let your hatred of me cause you to be reckless. I can reach you faster than the police. Ridge's words echoed in her mind. Had she messed up calling 911 instead of him?

When the sound of gunshots had awakened Ridge, he'd instantly started his truck and sped out of his hiding place at the edge of the property, driving across the front yard that was approximately the length of a football field.

Bang! Bang! Bang! Shots came from the backyard.

Stopping beside Jane's car, Ridge slammed his truck into Park and jumped out. A sharp pain shot up his leg. He grabbed his thigh and puffed out a breath. Then he pulled his weapon from its holster and raced along the side of the house, pushing his own discomfort to the back of his mind as he focused on the urgent matter before him. When he reached the back corner, he stopped and scanned the area. The full moon cast an ominous glow over the yard, and he could make out every detail of the patio, flower beds and lawn. However, shadows cloaked the area beyond that. The shooter could be behind the garden shed at the edge of the yard or anywhere in the trees that bordered the backyard.

Movement in the woods near the other end of the house caught his attention. His weapon at the ready, Ridge eased along the back of the house, careful to avoid anything that might cause him to trip and give away his location. He had hoped the shooter would make a run for it the moment he saw Ridge's headlights, making it easier for Ridge to spot him. Obviously, the assailant was too smart to fall for that.

Ridge was midway along the length of the house. Suddenly, a dark figure darted along the edge of the woods, shooting in his direction. Ducking behind a large potted plant, Ridge returned fire, he and the shooter exchanging multiple rounds in seconds.

The man disappeared around the side of the house. Ridge's heartbeat echoed the sound of his footsteps as he raced to cover the distance, desperate to stop the man before he disappeared in the night. Ridge rounded the corner, but the man wasn't in sight. He quickly scanned his surroundings as he charged to the front yard. Stepping around the corner, Ridge watched in horror as the shadow figure jumped into the truck Ridge had hastily exited moments before, the engine still running.

"Stop!" Ridge raised his weapon.

The shadow figure glanced his way, a white mask covering his face, and raised a hand in salute. Then he slammed the truck door and reversed down the drive. *A vehicle can be repaired. Don't let him escape. Shoot!*

Ridge shot at the retreating vehicle, hitting the front left headlight. The driver swung out of the driveway. Ridge fired once more, hitting the back passenger side window as the truck sped away. He gritted his teeth, and the vein in his neck twitched. How had he made such a rookie mistake? *Because Jane was the one in trouble. You let your emotions override your training.*

No time to worry about what he should have done differently. He had to get inside and check on Jane. Tamping down the frustration that welled inside him, he tucked his weapon into his waistband and raced up the porch steps. He wiggled the doorknob and banged on the door with his fist. "Jane!"

Narrow vertical windows covered with sheers framed the door. Ridge attempted to peer inside, but the entry was dark. No sound came from inside. He slammed his fist against the door, causing the frame to rattle. "Jane, can you hear me? It's Ridge! Let me in!"

Was she on the floor somewhere bleeding? He searched for a large rock or something he could use to bust out the window. A wrought iron plant stand, holding a potted fern, stood to the right of the door near a rocking chair. Quickly setting the fern on the porch, he grasped the top of the stand and prepared to use the legs to break the window so he could reach in and unlock the door. The front door flew open seconds before the metal connected with the glass.

"Ridge?" Jane stood framed in the entrance.

The metal stand clattered to the porch floor, and he guided Jane back into the house, closing the door behind them. "Are you hurt?"

"No." She shook her head. "There was a sound and… I looked out the window…and saw a small light beside the shed… I… It was the laser sight on his weapon…"

Her voice cracked, and he pulled her into his arms. "You're safe now. He's gone."

She pulled back and searched his face. "But why are you here? I called nine-one-one. Not you."

Ridge massaged his knee. He should have known sleeping in his truck would be bad on his old injury. "I never left. I parked at the edge of the property."

"You were guarding my house without telling me?"

"I'm sorry… Actually, no, I'm not. I had a bad feeling and couldn't leave you here alone." He straightened his shoulders. "I was being protective of a childhood friend. Someone who, at one time, was like family to me. And I'd do it all over again."

She closed her eyes and puffed out a breath, then she opened them again and met his gaze. "Thank you. For being here. Did you get the shooter?"

"No. Unfortunately, he got away." *In my truck.*

A siren pierced the air. Ridge pulled back the sheer covering the sidelight window and peered out. Two vehicles pulled into the drive. "Looks like the night patrol officer and Evan have both responded."

Jane gasped. "I need to get changed."

He glanced over his shoulder, taking in her appearance for the first time. She wore floral-print pajama pants and a T-shirt. "You're fine."

She frowned. "I don't need people I work with, especially my boss, to see me in my pj's."

"Okay. I'll go outside and meet them. Fill them in on what I know." He put a hand on the doorknob. "Stay inside. I'll bring them in after you've had time to change. Five minutes?"

"I only need three." She spun around and raced down the hall.

Ridge located the light switch next to the

door and flipped on the porch light. Then he stepped outside.

"Ridge, is Jane okay? Dispatch said there was a shooter." Evan met him at the foot of the steps. "And how are you here but your truck is on the side of the road, two miles away?"

Leave it to the sheriff to jump straight to the hardest question. Ridge may have let his guard down long enough for the shooter to steal his truck, but he would not make the same mistake twice. He would make it his mission to stay by Jane's side and protect her until the assailant was captured. Because there was no way Ridge would survive having another childhood friend lose their life on his watch.

THREE

Every inch of Jane's being ached as a fatigue unlike any she had ever experienced settled over her. Forcing her eyelids to open wider, she blinked several times and focused on the road ahead. She glanced at Ridge in her passenger seat, leaned back with his eyes closed. Despite his six-foot-two-inch frame, he seemed completely comfortable in her compact car.

Jane slowed and glanced in her rearview mirror. Evan was right behind her. She appreciated her boss's sense of duty and his desire to make sure she made it safely to Ridge's family's ranch, but she felt an immense amount of guilt at causing so much trouble for everyone. Realistically, she understood it was the police chief's job, but she'd always been a person who didn't want to cause others to be put out. Which was another reason she hadn't called Ridge earlier. Why would she wake him and pull him into the drama unfolding in her life when she could call the police? But now, here she was going to his family's ranch, and possibly leading a killer to their doorstep.

How did I let Ridge convince me this was a good idea? And why is he so determined to help me? I've been rude to him ever since Justin's funeral.

She really should stay somewhere else. But where? She couldn't go to her mom's house. *If the shooter hurt Mom...* Jane couldn't even think about that possibility. She sighed softly. There really wasn't anywhere else to go.

Activating her blinker, she turned onto the gravel drive. A large black iron sign proclaiming the property as Rustic Roots Ranch hung between two large timber posts.

"Zero, four, two, eight," Ridge said.

"What?" She stopped at the gate and turned to look at him.

"The passcode." He opened his eyes, smiled and pressed the button to raise the back of the seat to an upright position. "My parents' wedding anniversary. Even after all these years, my mom mourns what could have been."

Ridge had never really talked about his father much. Just that he died in a car accident after he and Ridge's mom got into a fight and he stormed out. She entered the code. After she cleared the entrance, the large black iron gate closed behind her.

Honk! Honk! Evan flashed his headlights and zoomed away. It was nearing sunrise, but she hoped he'd go home, grab a nap and then spend time with his children before heading to the office.

Memories of her and Justin playing basketball with their dad after he'd come home from work hit her out of nowhere. Her throat tightened as a flood of emotions assailed her. Would she ever get over missing her dad and brother? Some days, she still picked up the phone to call her dad to ask for advice or to text Justin and tell him something funny that had happened. She imagined the cell service provider had reassigned the numbers to new customers by now, but both their numbers were still in her contacts on her phone. And, even though she hadn't admitted it to Ridge earlier, she hadn't deleted his number, either. His mom wasn't the only one who mourned what could have been.

Scrubbing the back of her hand across her cheeks, she dried the silent tears that had fallen. *Pull yourself together. Otherwise, Ridge will think you're the same little sissy girl who used to cry when he pulled your pigtails.*

She drove past the main house. Darkness shrouded the majestic two-story stone and timber frame house. Its occupants most likely still slept. Ridge had said she could stay in the apartment above the barn. The three of them—Jane, Justin and Ridge—had spent many hours playing hide-and-seek in the barn when they were younger, but there hadn't been an apartment. Instead, the upstairs had been part hayloft and part open beams. Had he converted the hayloft into a studio apartment? Jane slowed as she neared the old red barn.

"There's a gravel road just ahead on the right. Turn there," Ridge instructed.

She followed his directions. Up on the hill, behind the main house, was a beautiful post and beam barn. There was a nice size parking area and a corral to the right of the barn. It seemed they'd made changes since her last visit. Of course, she hadn't been on the ranch since their high school graduation party. The night she'd finally been brave enough to kiss Ridge. And the night he flat-out rejected her, telling her she'd always be one of his best friends, but they would be nothing more.

I shouldn't have come here. There are too many memories. She would find another place once she had a few hours' sleep. Although, she doubted she would sleep. Jane bit her lower lip. Where could she stay that would be safe? Perhaps she could use the cabin on the Vincents' property, where Evan's wife, Grace, hid when her life was threatened several years ago.

Grace, who'd been a successful veterinary surgeon in Denver, had returned to Blackberry Falls to run her family's veterinary clinic. On the day of her return, she'd interrupted an intruder attempting to kill her sister, Chloe. When the would-be killer had turned his sights on Grace, Evan had protected her, securing the use of the remote cabin for her safety.

Jane didn't know the Vincent family well, but Evan did. She would talk to him about it.

She parked, exited the vehicle and grabbed her overnight bag out of the back seat. "This barn is beautiful. When did you build it?"

"Wyatt built it once he decided he wanted to offer equine therapy to special needs children. After Molly was born, it became his mission to make sure that she had the best life possible."

Ridge's five-year-old niece Molly—delivered six weeks prematurely due to an automobile accident that claimed her mother's life—had been born with congenital deafness. She was the happiest, most beautiful baby Jane had ever seen. It broke Jane's heart that Molly's mom, Ashlee, never held her child.

"So why is there an apartment upstairs in this barn?"

"Wyatt and Molly lived in it while he built

their new home. You can't see it from here. It's over near the apple orchard." Ridge reached for the overnight bag, and she handed it over. It was important to choose one's battles. Ridge's desire to be a gentleman wasn't an issue worth fighting over.

As she trailed behind Ridge, she thought of the beautiful two-story Victorian house Ashlee and Wyatt had lovingly restored downtown, near the town square. Ashlee had given Jane a tour of the home shortly after they'd purchased it. There had been four bedrooms, not counting the primary suite, and Ashlee had planned to fill every one of them with children. "I know some people love being an only child, but I always felt like I missed out by not having a brother or sister, or both. I don't want a child of mine to experience that," she'd said. Now, unless Wyatt remarried, Ashlee's daughter would be an only child.

"What about the house in town? Ashlee was so proud of the work they put into it."

"It was too hard for him to live there after Ashlee passed away. Too many memories." Ridge opened the door on the side of the barn and stepped back to allow Jane to enter. "He has a renter living in it at the moment, but I wouldn't be surprised if he sells it in the near future."

She entered the spacious barn. There were stalls lining the center aisle that was lit by several well-placed night-lights. Immediately to her left was a set of stairs with a wrought iron railing. The craftsmanship of the barn was stunning, but she'd expect nothing less of the Snyder family.

Jane couldn't imagine having roots that went as deep as Ridge's family. The ranch property had been in Eleanor Snyder's family for seven generations. When her father, Silas Ramsey, passed away, he'd left the land to Eleanor— his only child—and her two sons. Since, Ridge and Wyatt had both built homes on the ranch, it was obvious they planned to carry on their family legacy.

"Are you coming?"

Pulled from her thoughts, Jane was startled to see Ridge halfway up the staircase. "Oh, sorry." She scrambled up the stairs behind him and followed him into a spacious apartment. "It's beautiful."

"Yeah. Wyatt has always been a master craftsman. It almost seems a waste that he spends all his time training horses and teaching little children to ride."

She moved farther into the apartment, looking around. The kitchen, living and dining area were on one side, and tucked into an alcove area was a small bedroom area. To the right of that was a door that she assumed led to the bathroom. "I don't disagree with your assessment, but maybe

Wyatt is afraid he wouldn't enjoy building beautiful things if he had to make a living at it. This way, building and woodworking becomes a hobby that he can enjoy in his spare time."

"You could be right." Ridge dropped the overnight bag on the sofa and turned to her. "What time do you have to be at the station?"

"I don't. Evan told me to take the day off, so I will probably sleep until noon."

"What about the college? You have a class tonight?"

"Yes. At six. Why?" *Please, don't offer to go with me.*

"I wanted to know what time to be ready." He met her gaze.

His blue eyes, flecked with gold, caused her heart to do a fluttery flip, just as they had throughout high school. Her throat tightened, and for a moment, she forgot how to breathe.

"I'll see you at four thirty. We'll stop by the diner for an early dinner before heading to campus." He tipped his head and turned to the door.

"Wait!" she exclaimed, a little too loudly.

He turned to face her, one eyebrow raised.

She swallowed. "There's no need for you to disrupt your schedule more than you already have. I can drive myself to campus."

"You need someone with you. To protect you." He took a step toward her. "I know there's no point trying to convince you not to go to work this evening, but I won't sit back and watch you put yourself into a dangerous situation without backup."

"I'll notify campus security. An officer can walk me to my vehicle."

"And what about the drive to and from campus? There's a long stretch of road where the shooter could ambush you."

Now was as good a time as any to tell him her plans. "I thought I'd ask Evan to make other arrangements for my temporary accommodations. He can—"

"Do you hate me that much?" Each word— though barely above a whisper—landed with a thud. Ridge leaned in.

"Don't you understand? This is something I can't walk away from. I have to be the one to protect you. I owe it to Justin. Please, can't you let me be the one to watch over you?"

She inhaled sharply. The agony in his eyes tore at her soul. How could she say *no* without seeming heartless? But she wasn't sure she was strong enough to move beyond the past and let Ridge back into her life, even if it meant keeping her alive.

The muscle in Ridge's jaw twitched as he waited for her to respond to his request. No, it was more than a request. It was a plea. She had to have heard it in his voice. Just like he could see all of Jane's emotions as they raced through her head.

She'd always had an expressive face. It was one of the things he liked most about her. And the thing that had caused him the greatest pain when he'd had to tell her they would never be more than friends. He'd wanted to say so much more that evening, but he couldn't. How could he have explained that the kiss had been everything he'd dreamed it would be—on the rare occasions in high school when he'd let his guard down and allowed himself to dream of Jane being more than a friend—and still turn her away?

Thankfully, he'd mustered the strength to bridle in his emotions, even though every part of him had wanted to cling to her and never let her go. If he had admitted his feelings that night, there's no way he could have ever walked away from her. He would have begged her to give up everything and become a military spouse. And Ridge had been determined not to follow in his parents' footsteps. They married young, and the stress of military life had contributed to the many fights during their union.

Ridge would not have been able to live with himself if he'd followed his heart and pursued a relationship with Jane, only to have a tumultuous marriage like his parents. Some people just weren't suited for marriage, and Ridge was one of them. He'd known that for a long time. How could he expect to be a good husband when he'd never witnessed the example of one? His mom may have idealized her marriage to his dad, but Ridge had seen the raw truth. As early as eight years of age, he'd known his parents' relationship was not a healthy one. The constant bickering, slamming of doors and his dad's routine disappearing act.

Not allowing himself to pursue a relationship with Jane had been best. Ridge had no doubt, if they'd married, their union would not have withstood Justin's death, especially with Jane blaming him for everything.

"Okay," she whispered, pulling him from his thoughts.

"What?" Had he heard her correctly?

"I said, okay. You can be my bodyguard. You do *owe it* to Justin. If he were here, he'd protect me. But remember, once Evan catches the shooter, we go back to the way things were. You go your way. I go mine. This is not an invitation to renew our friendship."

Even without the words, he read her expression, loud and clear. "I understand." *You will never forgive me. But that's okay, because I'll never forgive myself, either.*

"One more thing." She folded her arms across her stomach, as if she were bracing for an argument. "You can't be in my classroom. You'll have to—"

"I can't protect you if I'm not allowed to stay with you."

"If the shooter wanted to attack while there were people around, he wouldn't have waited until I was alone on campus last night. Semester exams are stressful enough without having a stranger in the room." She pinned him with her gaze. "You can wait in my office. Two doors down from my classroom."

"What if—"

"My teaching assistant will be with me the entire time. And I'll come to my office as soon as the last student has completed their exam." She dropped her arms and squared her shoulders, a determined glint in her eyes.

He didn't want to argue with her, not after she'd just agreed to his protection. It had been a long night. She was tired—they both were— and defensive. The discussion on where he was stationed while guarding her could wait until they'd both had a few hours of sleep.

He pressed his lips. "I'll get out of here so you can get some rest. Coffee, bottled water, protein bars and snacks are in the kitchen. Help yourself."

"Thank you."

Ridge tipped his head. "I'll ask Wyatt to keep the noise level down in the barn this morning. And I'll have food supplies delivered this afternoon."

"Please don't ask anyone to take time to shop for me. We can stop at the grocery store this evening, and I can get what I need."

"It's no bother. I've turned a small section of the ranch into a hobby farm. Complete with laying hens, cows, goats and a garden. Plenty of fresh ingredients for whatever meal you crave. If you need anything else, we'll stop at the store on the way home." He walked out of the apartment and closed the door before she could reply. Typical Jane. As long as he'd known her, she'd never wanted to be a bother to anyone. He wished he could make her understand that helping her was not and never would be a bother.

Click. Ridge smiled at the sound of the deadbolt locking, thankful she was taking her safety seriously. He jogged down the stairs and out the side door, running smack-dab into his brother.

"Whoa." Wyatt put his palms on Ridge's chest, preventing them both from toppling over. "I thought you were off chasing some guy who skipped bail. What are you doing in the barn at this time of morning? And who's MINI Cooper is that?" Wyatt slung questions at him in rapid succession.

Ridge looked around. The sun barely peeked above the mountain to the east, streaks of orange, red, yellow and purple colored the sky. "I didn't realize it was so late."

"Late? Don't you mean early?" Wyatt asked, one eyebrow raised.

"Let's go over here." Ridge crossed to the edge of the corral, turned and glanced up at the apartment windows. The light went out. Hopefully, that meant Jane was going to bed.

"Where is your truck?" Wyatt nodded at Jane's car. "Whose car is that?"

"My truck is at the police impound yard being checked for fingerprints, though I'm sure Evan is wasting his time since the person who stole it wore gloves."

"You saw them?" Wyatt's eyes rounded.

"Yes. As for the car, it belongs to Jane Mason. I told her she could stay in the loft apartment."

"What? I thought she wasn't talking to you? Doesn't she still blame you for Justin's death?"

"Yes," Ridge acknowledged. "This is a temporary truce. One of necessity."

"Okay. Tell me what happened."

"Jane is working with Evan to solve the Brush Hollow Reservoir Murders."

"I read about that. Her aunt was one of the victims."

"Yes." Ridge looked at Wyatt, meeting his eyes. "It seems the murderer isn't too happy the case is being revisited. He attacked Jane as she was leaving her classroom last evening. She escaped but then he showed up at her house and tried again. Thankfully, I was able to scare him away. But—"

"You were there?" Wyatt scratched the back of his head. "I'm so confused."

Ridge inhaled deeply and puffed the air out. "Never mind that. I just need you to work quietly in the barn this morning. Jane has had no sleep. I'd like her to get a few hours of rest since she's determined to go administer the final exam to her students tonight."

Wyatt looked as if he wanted to ask more questions but thought better of it. He nodded. "No problem. I don't have any riding classes until the afternoon. After I feed and water the horses, I'm headed up to the main house to have breakfast with Molly and Mom. Molly has a doctor's appointment at nine. They're doing allergy testing today, and I promised her a trip to the toy store afterward." A frown crossed his face. "I hate seeing her poked with needles."

If there was any way Ridge could alleviate some of his younger brother's stress, he would happily do so. But he'd learned a long time ago that people had to work through their own issues, in their own time. Being a single parent of a special needs child was a heavy load to bear, but Ridge was sure Wyatt knew he was there for him anytime he needed to talk. Being two years older, growing up, he'd tried to shield Wyatt from the harsh realities of life. Before their father died in a car accident, anytime their parents would get into a verbal fight—which normally took place behind a closed bedroom door, though it did little to muffle their voices—Ridge would take Wyatt into the living room, put his favorite cartoon movie on the television, turn the volume up and grab a box of sugary cereal out of the kitchen. Then he would make a fort using a blanket and the pillows off the couch. They would sit in the fort, eating cereal by the handfuls and block out the rest of the world.

Too bad a blanket fort and a box of cereal wouldn't be enough to protect Jane from the evil lurking on her doorstep. Whatever it took to keep her safe, he would be there…a shield between her and the killer after her.

FOUR

For the second time in ten hours, Ridge was in Jane's vehicle with her. Only this time, he'd asked if he could drive, so he was behind the wheel and she was in the passenger seat. Thankfully, as it normally did, a heating pad and muscle pain cream had reduced the pain in his leg to a dull ache. Ninety percent of the time, he didn't have any issues with his knee. It was only when he spent too long riding in a vehicle or sitting or squatting in one place that it gave him issues, causing his entire leg to hurt. Which was why he'd been medically discharged from the military. Navy SEALs had to be at their best one hundred percent of the time.

"Did Evan say when you could have your truck back?" Jane asked, breaking into his thoughts.

"Tomorrow afternoon." He merged into the roundabout, taking the second exit that led to the faculty parking deck. "But I must say, this is a fun vehicle to drive. Maybe I should trade my truck in for one of these."

She giggled. "You'd look real cute driving with hay strapped to the roof of a MINI Cooper."

"Yeah, I guess it wouldn't be very practical for the ranch." He activated the blinker, turned into the parking deck, rolled down his window, accepted the faculty ID badge she held out to him and scanned it. The metal arm blocking the entrance lifted, and he pulled through.

She shivered. "I hate parking decks. They're so creepy, especially at night."

"Is that why you told me you normally park in the open parking areas?"

"Yes," she replied.

"I believe it will be easier to protect you here than it would be out in the open. Besides, I'm with you today, so you don't have to be afraid of the dark parking deck." He pulled into a parking spot three spaces from the door and slid the gearshift into Park. "Stay put. I'll come around and open your door."

"There's no need for you to be a gentleman, I'm perfectly capab—"

"For safety reasons." He put a hand on her arm, halting her from opening the door. "I need a chance to look around before you get out in the open."

"Oh."

Was that disappointment in her voice? Had she thought he was opening her door as an act of chivalry? Which he most definitely would do, if this were a date. *This most definitely wasn't a date*. He was only trying to do his duty by Justin and keep Jane alive. That was all.

Only, he'd temporarily forgotten he was simply the bodyguard while they ate dinner at Josie's Diner. Sitting in a booth with Jane across from him had been like old times. Well, almost. Justin's absence had been achingly obvious. But then the food had arrived, and they'd slipped into casual conversation, with him asking about her photography classes and listening as she gave animated replies. It was apparent she enjoyed teaching.

He exited the vehicle and scanned the area. They were on the ground level of the four-level parking deck, in the section designated for faculty.

"Remember, she hates you. Rightly so. If you hadn't convinced Justin joining the Navy would be the adventure of a lifetime, he would still be alive. And she knows it," he mumbled. Leaning over slightly, he opened her door.

Jane's brow furrowed. "Did you say something?"

"Nothing. Just talking to myself." Heat crept up his neck. He hadn't intended for her to hear him.

"Oh." She reached into the back seat and grasped her satchel. Then she climbed out of the car, and he closed the door behind her.

He really hated not being able to carry his weapon with him into the building, but he had to obey the law. So he had locked his handgun in a pistol lockbox he'd stashed under her passenger seat. He could remove it from the box once they left campus and have it to protect her as they drove back to the ranch, if needed. If trouble hit while on campus, he'd have to rely on his hand-to-hand combat training.

"Stay close." Ridge lightly grasped her elbow and hurried her into the building.

Jane pulled free of his hold. "I know you're only trying to keep me safe, but I can walk— beside you—unaided."

He clenched his teeth, and a muscle in his jaw twitched. How could he protect her if she recoiled every time he touched her? "You're right. I don't want you to be an easy target. By having you as close to my side as possible, I can use my body to block yours."

"From bullets?"

"Yes. If I get hit, I need you to react quickly. Don't worry about me. Run, for your life."

She blanched, nodded and glanced away. Ridge hated to be graphic, but he needed her to understand the seriousness of the situation. The killer had shot at her twice and would do it again. The more times the man targeting her shot, the better his chances of hitting his mark and killing her.

The elevator doors opened, and Jane scurried inside, her face flushed. Ridge entered behind her, and she leaned over and pushed the second-floor button. As soon as the doors closed, she pressed as close as she could to the wall, putting space between them. His words must have affected her more than he thought they had.

"Is that what happened in combat? Did the rest of the squad abandon an injured soldier, fleeing for their lives and leaving him bleeding on the ground?" she whispered, raw anger echoing in her voice.

So that was what had hit a nerve. Ridge had long wanted to tell her about the ambush the day Justin died, and how he'd tried so hard to save him. But this wasn't the time or place. He leaned against the back wall and looked straight ahead.

In his peripheral vision, he saw Jane close her eyes, her chest rising and falling as she took slow breaths in and out. The elevator lurched and moved upward. In a matter of seconds, they had reached the second floor. The doors opened, revealing a man in his mid-fifties. A short-lived look of surprise registered on his face before he shuttered his expression.

The man stepped aside. "Good evening, Jane."

"Good evening, Dean Gibson," she replied, straightening her stance.

Ridge slid his hand down her arm and laced his fingers with hers. Then he walked out of the elevator, ensuring she stayed close to his side.

Dean Gibson cleared his throat. "Who is your *friend*?"

"Oh." She glanced from the man to Ridge. A confused look on her face.

Was she wondering how to introduce him? They weren't really friends any longer, but they were much more than acquaintances. And she definitely couldn't say he was her bodyguard without provoking a lot of questions.

Ridge met the older man's gaze. "Ridge Snyder. Jane's childhood friend."

"Allen Gibson." The man held out his hand. "Nice to meet you."

Reluctantly, Ridge released Jane's hand and accepted the handshake. Dean Gibson tightened his grip as if he were playing a childish game of who's stronger, where each person attempted to bring the other to their knees. The muscle in Ridge's jaw twitched. Acutely aware of Jane staring, Ridge subtly increased the pressure of his grip to show the other man he wasn't intimidated.

The large metal doors began to close, and Dean Gibson stuck his free hand into the opening to stop them. Releasing Ridge's hand, he smiled at Jane and stepped inside the elevator. "Have a nice evening."

"You, too, sir," Jane replied as the doors closed.

"He was an interesting person." Ridge massaged his hand. "His grip was firm. What is he the dean of, anyway? Physical education?"

She grinned. "Well, he does work out regularly and is a marathon runner. But his job title is dean of students. He oversees the academic side of things, as well as handling any disciplinary issues or student complaints."

Jane led the way down the hall. A couple of female students were sitting on the floor outside her classroom door, so she paused and unlocked the door. "You can go inside. I need to stop by my office, but I'll be back shortly."

The girls scrambled to their feet—large portfolios clutched in their hands—as they stared at Ridge.

He smiled at them. "Hello."

"Hi," the girls said in unison, huge grins on their faces as they disappeared into the room.

Ridge scratched the side of his head. "What was that all about?"

"Oh, come on. I'm sure you're used to females finding you attractive."

He furrowed his brow, a frown on his face. "I'll admit, I've had women flirt with me, but that was different."

"They're nineteen-year-olds. They've not mastered the art of flirting." She touched his arm. "Come on, let's get you settled in my office."

"Have you?" he asked as he followed her, stopping in front of the second door past her room.

Jane unlocked the door, turned on the light and walked into the room that wasn't much larger than a broom closet. A desk took up most of the space. There was a small window behind it, and a single armchair squeezed in front of it.

"Have I, what?" she asked, turning to come face-to-face with his chest.

"Have you—" he leaned down and whispered, her hair blowing as he spoke "—mastered the art of flirting?"

A pink hue colored her cheeks. It was as much fun getting a rise out of her now as it had been in high school. Her unawareness of her own beauty had always amazed him. When she blushed, she instantly went from wholesome girl-next-door to a stunningly beautiful woman.

"Stop." Jane waved her hand, brushing him away. "We're not kids anymore. I won't fall for your teasing."

Teasing? More like curiosity. Did she have a boyfriend? He hadn't heard mention of one since returning home, but then again, his mom and brother always changed the subject if Jane's name came up.

"My class shouldn't last longer than a couple of hours," Jane continued, pulling him back to the present. "The portfolio presentations will only take about ninety minutes. I'll give the students a ten-minute break and then they'll complete the written test. Some will finish quickly, but I doubt it takes anyone over forty minutes."

"Are you still convinced I shouldn't sit in the back of your classroom?"

She narrowed her eyes. "Are you serious? You saw the way Alyssa and Claudia acted. I can't have my students distracted during their final exam."

He wanted to argue with her, but he couldn't. It might be for the best, anyway. Her first encounter with the shooter took place on this floor. Maybe he could spend the time looking for clues. "Okay, but I'm walking you to your classroom. And I'll do regular patrols of the area." Ridge nodded to her desktop computer. "May I use your computer to access the internet? I'd like to research old newspaper articles to see what was going on in Blackberry Falls the weeks leading up to the murders."

"Like what?"

"Were there an unusual number of break-ins or did anyone go missing? I'm just looking to gather whatever information I can to help pinpoint who the killer is." He shook his head. "I don't know. But I'll feel like I'm being productive while I wait and the time will pass more quickly...or at least it will seem like it."

Jane moved behind her desk, leaned over the chair and typed on the keyboard. "I'll also turn off the auto-sleep function so the computer will stay logged in if you walk away for a few minutes." She straightened. "Okay, it's time for me to get to class."

Nervous energy welled inside him, just as it always had before a SEAL mission. He released a breath. "Would you mind if I say a prayer first?"

"What good—" She met his eyes and pressed her lips into a frown.

He'd heard Jane had stopped attending church services soon after Justin's death. It broke his heart to think she'd turned from God instead of clinging to Him in times of trouble. Ridge knew Justin would be sad his death had caused a rift in Jane's relationship with the Lord.

"Justin always asked to lead us in prayer before our team went into a dangerous situation," Ridge said softly, not breaking eye contact. "This feels just as dangerous as any mission I've ever taken part in...because I care about the person in danger."

Tears rimmed her eyes. A few seconds passed. She nodded and bowed her head.

Ridge clasped his hands in front of him and bowed. "Our most holy and heavenly Father, thank you for all the blessings You've granted us in this life. I come to You at this time to ask for safety for Jane and for clarity for us both as we work together to catch a killer..."

Jane glanced up from the stack of exams she'd been grading. Only one student remained. Summer Fisher. Jane wasn't surprised it was taking her longer than the others.

Jane had been Summer's faculty advisor ever since she enrolled as a freshman the previous fall. Even though this was Jane's first time having Summer in class, Jane had met with her several times the previous semester to discuss her academic struggles. And they'd formed a strong bond. As a result, it had been Jane who'd first suspected Summer had a learning difference. Thankfully, Summer had gone to her parents with Jane's concerns and they'd pursued every avenue to help their child, leading to her diagnosis of dyslexia.

Summer looked up and smiled. She put her pencil in her purse, stood and brought the exam to Jane. "I'm sorry, Professor Mason. I didn't realize I was the last person." Summer looked around. "Even Beth has gone?"

Jane's teaching assistant often suffered from severe migraines. When she'd complained of a blinding headache earlier, Jane had sent her home to rest.

"Yes. She wasn't feeling well." Jane reached for the exam paper. "I'm glad you took your time and didn't feel rushed. How do you think you did?"

"I aced it." Summer's face lit up.

It seemed Summer's newfound confidence was making her overly confident. Jane hoped the girl hadn't made careless mistakes on her test. "I look forward to grading it. I will have all grades posted by Monday."

"Thank you, Professor Mason." Summer walked toward the door, waving goodbye. "Have a good evening."

"You, too, Summer."

Jane looked around her classroom and sighed. "Guess it's time to go."

She would have loved to hang out in her classroom just a little longer and finish grading papers, but she couldn't. Ridge had made her promise she'd come to her office as soon as the last student left so he could drive her back to the ranch. Standing, she gathered the test papers and shoved them into her satchel with her laptop.

"Lord, please let us catch the murderer soon," she whispered, heading toward the door. Jane stopped in her tracks. Where had that come from? Had Ridge's prayer earlier been the trigger?

Jane had stopped praying and going to church after Mrs. Cannon told her at Justin's funeral that his death was "God's will." How could it have been His will that Justin would die at twenty-six? Justin had not lived long enough to marry or have children or grow old. If that was God's will, then she did not want to go to church. Even her mom's pleading hadn't convinced her to resume attendance.

This wasn't the time to examine her sudden urge to pray. Ridge was waiting for her. She crossed to the door and stepped out into the hall. Summer had already disappeared, and no one else was in the hall. The classroom adjacent to Jane's room was dark, the door closed, but a few of the other classrooms still had lights on. Good, she wasn't the last one to leave this evening.

She turned toward her office, then changed directions and ducked into the ladies' restroom. The prayer had shaken her more than she wanted to admit. She needed a minute to compose herself. Pushing open the restroom door, she stepped inside, almost bumping into a young woman with oversized glasses and curly hair. "Sorry."

The girl smiled and scurried out of the room. Jane crossed to the sinks. The mauve-colored Formica countertops with stained porcelain sinks begged for a makeover. Jane doubted such a remodel was a top priority for the college expense fund. At least, the janitorial service prided itself on keeping the restrooms clean and well stocked.

She dropped her satchel on the counter-top and turned on the cold-water faucet. Then she leaned over, cupped her hands under the running water, capturing what she could, and splashed her face. The cool water instantly soothing her nervous system. The door rattled. Straightening, she held her hand under the towel dispenser and watched, but the door never opened. Whoever it was must have changed their mind about entering.

Jane tore the section of paper towel, dabbed her face and tossed the paper in the trash. Then she glanced in the mirror. "The sooner you solve this case, the sooner you can go back to your normal life. No more being around Ridge. Or having to hear his prayers. Just working, taking photos when you want and doing your own thing."

Stepping toward the door, she scrunched her nose. What was that sickeningly sweet smell? Jane turned around in a semicircle, trying to follow the scent. A yellowish fog flowed out of the air vents near the ceiling. Pressing a hand over her nose, she narrowed her eyes. What was that?

Beep, beep, beep! Beep, beep, beep! The deafening shrills of the smoke alarm sounded, followed by the sound of people yelling and running in the hall. Jane whirled around, grasped the door handle with her free hand and tugged. It didn't budge. She pulled harder. Nothing. Holding her breath, she dropped her other hand to the door handle. Grasping it two-handed, she jerked the handle as hard as she could.

I'm locked in! Panic welled inside her. There were no windows in the room. How was she going to get out?

Puffing out the breath she'd been holding, she pounded on the steel door with the sides of her fists. "Help! I'm locked inside! Someone, please, help!"

Nausea welled inside her, and a feeling of faintness enveloped her. Suddenly unable to stand, she sank to the floor. Her limbs were heavy, as if they were weighted down by a pile of quilts. Mustering all the energy she could, she lifted her hands and slapped them against the door. They barely made a sound. *I'm going to die.*

The door lurched beneath her hands.

"Jane!" Ridge yelled. "Are you in there?"

"Ridge," she cried. "I'm locked in." Tears burned the backs of her eyes. *Please, Lord, let him get me out.*

Something slammed against the door and it rattled. "Hrmph." Ridge's grunt verified it was his body that had connected with the door. "I have to get help. I'll be right back."

"Hurry." Jane pressed her cheek against the cool metal door. "There's gas or something coming through the vents."

Silence followed. Had he heard her plea before he went for help? She glanced around. A dense haze filled the small room. "I need to move so I'm not blocking the door," she mumbled to herself. "Ridge *will* get it open. He won't leave me trapped in here."

Jane crawled on her hands and knees to the opposite wall. Dropping to the floor, she curled her body into the fetal position and covered her head with her forearms, her breathing labored. *Please, hurry. Before I die.*

FIVE

Beep, beep, beep! Beep, beep, beep! Ridge attempted to block out the sound of the alarm as he watched the custodian pull a broken key out of the bathroom door lock using a type of tweezers. The man, a good five inches taller than Ridge's six feet two inches, wearing coveralls with the name Carl stitched in the upper right-hand corner, stood and dropped the small piece of metal into Ridge's outstretched hand.

"Hurry, open the door. We need to get her out of there," Ridge urged. He hadn't been able to get a response from Jane for the past five minutes.

Carl pulled the retractable keychain attached to his belt and quickly selected a key, then he inserted it into the lock and opened the door. Ridge pushed past him and into the room. A wave of noxious gas assailed him and he coughed.

"What in the world?" Carl covered his mouth

with the crook of his arm, crossed to the vent, reached up and closed it, stemming the flow of fumes.

Jane lay in a heap on the floor. Ridge swooped her into his arms and raced out of the room.

"Call nine-one-one," Ridge yelled over his shoulder to Carl, who was following close behind. "Tell them we need an ambulance."

Thankfully, all the other occupants of the building were already outside, and the hallway was now empty. As the trio neared the stairwell, Carl brushed past Ridge, his cell phone to his ear as he explained the situation to the 911 operator, and opened the door. Holding Jane firmly against his chest, Ridge sprinted down the stairs.

Reaching the first-floor landing, Ridge stepped back to allow the custodian to open the door. As he did so, the bullet hole in the doorframe caught his eye. Anger welled inside him. Jane had been in this same stairwell last night, running from the killer as he shot at her. And now she was being carried out unconscious. Was the killer behind the fire alarm? He had to be. No one else would have broken a key off in the lock. And there'd been no smoke or gas anywhere other than the women's restroom.

Ridge shouldn't have allowed Jane to come to the campus tonight. *How could you have stopped her? You have no right to tell her what to do.*

"An ambulance is on the way," Carl informed Ridge as he went around him to open the front door.

"Thank you." Ridge stepped outside, where crowds of people stood in clusters, talking and staring at the building.

A husky man of average height, wearing wire-rimmed glasses rushed over to him. "What happened to Professor Mason? Is she okay?"

"She's fine Professor Smythe," Carl replied before Ridge could. "Just inhaled too much smoke. An ambulance is coming. Give us room, so she can get fresh air."

Professor Smythe backed away as others moved forward to join him and gawk.

"Move back, everyone. Nothing to see here." The custodian used his hands to shoo the people away.

Ridge glanced up at him. "Thank you."

"No problem." He nodded toward Jane, concern etched in his eyes. "Is she okay?"

"I think so." Ridge laid Jane on a bench and knelt beside her, watching as her chest rose and fell. "Her breathing is steady."

Sirens rent the air. Ridge pushed to his feet

as two fire trucks and an ambulance screeched to a stop in front of the building.

"Stay with her," Carl ordered. "I'll direct the medics over here."

Ridge nodded and moved to stand behind the bench, his eyes darting around the crowd. The killer was most likely out here watching, waiting to see if his plan had worked. Scanning the men's faces, he could easily rule out 70 percent of them because they weren't even alive when the murders occurred. That left Professor Smythe and five other men, whom Ridge did not know.

"What happened to Jane?" a familiar-sounding voice asked from behind.

Ridge turned and watched as Dean Gibson walked toward him, coming from the faculty parking deck area. Dressed casually in jeans and a T-shirt with the school logo emblazoned on it, it appeared he'd come from home. Had someone called him to tell him about the fire alarm? He must live close to have gotten here so quickly.

"She inhaled too much smoke," Ridge replied.

Dean Gibson glanced at the building. "I don't see any flames. And when Professor Clinton called me to report the alarm, he said he didn't smell any smoke."

"She's right here," Carl declared, guiding the EMTs to the bench.

"How long has she been unconscious?" a woman about his and Jane's age carrying a red medic bag asked.

"I'm not sure." Ridge furrowed his brow. "Anywhere from ten to fifteen minutes."

The woman and her male partner immediately went to work checking Jane's vitals.

"Heart rate sixty-two. BP one hundred sixteen over sixty," the woman said.

"O2 sat eighty-nine," the man declared. "No signs of broken bones or contusions. Let's transport."

"I'm coming with you," Ridge declared.

"You can't ride with us," the woman said as she wrapped her hands around Jane's ankles and nodded at her partner, who had his hands under Jane's shoulders.

"Lift," the male medic instructed. They lifted in unison and quickly transitioned Jane to the gurney they'd wheeled over when they walked up.

Ridge pushed past Dean Gibson and rounded the bench. "I have to—"

"You can follow us," the male medic said. "But you're not riding in the ambulance."

Ridge felt Jane's pockets and located her

phone. "Her phone is on her. If anything at all happens, call me. Name is Ridge Snyder."

"Rustic Roots Ranch?" the man asked.

"Yeah."

"My daughter takes riding lessons there." The man met Ridge's eyes. "We'll take good care of her. See you at the ER." Then he turned to his partner. "Let's go."

They wheeled Jane down the sidewalk to the ambulance. Dreading letting Jane out of his sight, Ridge stayed rooted in place until they loaded her and closed the doors.

"Want a lift to the hospital?" Dean Gibson asked.

"No. I have a vehicle. And I doubt Jane would want her coworkers there. I'm sure you know she's a very private person." Thankful he'd parked on the first level, Ridge raced to the parking deck.

He was in Jane's car and pulling out of the parking deck before the ambulance exited the campus. Pressing down on the gas, he bounced over a speed bump. *Ugh.* For a split second, he'd forgotten he wasn't in his truck. Easing off the pedal, he inched over each subsequent bump. When he reached the exit, the ambulance was no longer in sight. Ridge pulled his phone out of his back pocket and gave the voice-command to call Evan Bradshaw.

Dear Lord, please let Evan have an officer near the hospital so they can guard Jane until I get there. Ridge puffed out a sigh. *Do I need the police to take over her protection? No! I let her down. Lord, please don't let her die. I will stick to her like glue from here on out. She will not get out of my sight.*

"She should wake up soon," a soft-spoken female voice penetrated Jane's consciousness.

"We'll wait as long as it takes," a male responded.

Where was she? And why were these people talking while she was sleeping? *Aaah.* Her head was pounding. She tried to open her eyes, but her eyelids felt like someone had glued them shut. "I…need…"

"Jane," Ridge breathed huskily, near her ear. "What do you need?"

"Give me some room, please," the female voice said, her tone stern.

There were sounds of movement. Jane forced her eyes open. Then closed them instantly, the florescent lighting too bright. "Ah." She moistened her lips. "Where am I?"

Why did her throat hurt? She lifted a hand to rub it and something tugged at her skin.

"Careful, or you'll pull out your IV," the female cautioned, gently guiding her arm down until it connected with the mattress.

IV? She was in the hospital. The memories came flooding back to her. She gasped and opened her eyes, squinting against the light. "Did he…was he…"

"Shhh. We can talk about what happened later. Right now, let's just get you better." Ridge's hand clasped hers as he offered her a closed-lipped smile. It was the kind of smile one gave to people when they wanted them to believe everything was okay, when it really wasn't.

Jane glanced around the small space—pale yellow walls on three sides and taupe-colored curtains across the front, separating it from the nurses' station. The nurse, a petite woman with brown hair arranged in a tidy bun at the base of her neck—reminiscent of a nurse on an old medical drama—was checking Jane's vitals on the monitor. Ridge pressed against the bed on the opposite side, while Evan leaned against the wall behind him, taking everything in.

She met Ridge's eyes. "How did you get me out?"

"I didn't. Carl did."

Jane thought of the quiet giant of a custodian. He was one of the sweetest men she'd ever known. At age seventy-three, he was long past retirement age, but he still worked three days a week, covering the evening shift—his preference—with a smile for each person he came in contact with. The students and faculty all loved him. Now, it seemed she owed him her life.

"Your vitals look good," the nurse smiled at Jane. "I'll let Dr. Davis know you're awake." She slipped between the curtains and disappeared.

Jane pressed the button on the side rail of the hospital bed to raise her head. Once she was sitting more upright, she inhaled a deep breath of the cool air being supplied by the nasal cannula, then released it slowly. "So, how did the killer lock me inside? And what was the gas being pumped into the bathroom through the vents?"

"He broke a key off in the lock." Ridge caressed the back of her hand with his thumb. "Thankfully, Carl knew how to extract it quickly."

"I'm still wondering how he had the right tools on him at that exact moment." Evan crossed to the bed. "Most custodians don't walk around with a tool belt on."

"He had a Leatherman tool in his pocket," Ridge replied.

Evan furrowed his brow. "You don't think that was kind of convenient?"

Jane gasped. "You can't seriously think Carl

is the killer. If he were, why would he have freed me so quickly? Wouldn't it have served his purpose to leave me in there long enough to die?"

"She has a point," Ridge acknowledged.

"Still, I'm not ready to rule anyone out just yet," Evan replied.

"Ms. Mason." A tall, slender woman with short blond hair entered the room. "I'm Dr. Davis." She looked from Jane to the men standing on either side of the bed. "We normally only allow one visitor with patients in the ER. Chief Bradshaw, are you here on official police business?"

"Jane has been the target of a series of attacks. She's also a member of the police department," Evan answered. "So, I'm here as her friend and her boss. And Ridge is..." He glanced at Jane. "...a childhood friend who is lending a hand while the investigation is ongoing."

Dr. Davis gave a slight nod. Then, after checking the IV and glancing at the monitor, she turned to Jane and smiled. "Would you like the men to step outside while we talk?"

Jane looked from Ridge to Evan. She didn't imagine there was any reason for them to step outside, as whatever the doctor had to say concerning the lab results would go in the police report. "No. They can stay."

"Fine. Your blood pressure is good. Your heart rate is steady. And your oxygen levels have improved significantly." Dr. Davis opened her electronic tablet and typed on the screen, then she looked up. "All of your labs look good."

The doctor looked at Evan. "Since you indicated this was the result of a crime, I can order further testing. It could take days to get the results."

"Please, do. Even if you don't believe the gas Jane inhaled negatively affected her, we will need all the evidence possible to prosecute the culprit after his arrest."

After his arrest. Would they catch him? Or would Jane become another victim? Nikki and Phoebe had died from strangulation. But the killer had shot at Jane twice and now attempted to poison her with some type of gas. It didn't seem like he had a preferred method of killing—his only goal being death, to whomever he deemed a threat. And unlike the night before, he hadn't hesitated to attack with others on campus. What if the other girl hadn't exited the bathroom before he jammed the lock? Had he known Jane was alone in the restroom? Or was he willing to kill others just to get to her?

Ridge rubbed her arm. She met his eyes.

Don't, he mouthed and shook his head. Jane furrowed her brow. Don't what? Could Ridge tell she was feeling guilt over putting others in danger? She doubted it. Maybe at one time, years ago, he could read her body language and know her thoughts but those days were long gone.

"Does this mean I can go home?" *No, not home. I won't be going back there until the killer after me has been caught.* "You said my oxygen has improved," Jane added hopefully.

"It has." Dr. Davis furrowed her brows. "You should be okay at home—"

"Oh, thank you!" Jane exclaimed.

"But only if you check your oxygen levels often throughout the night," Dr. Davis inserted firmly. "If it drops below ninety-two, I want you to come straight back to the emergency room. Understand?"

Jane turned to Ridge. "I don't have a pulse oximeter."

"I'll call Wyatt. I'm sure he has one. After Molly was born, he stocked his medicine cabinet with all the gadgets."

"It's best for her to use one designed for an adult," Dr. Davis interjected.

Ridge smiled at her. "I'll be surprised if my

brother doesn't have one. But if not, we'll pick one up."

"Okay, then. I'll start the discharge paperwork."

Two hours later, Jane rode in the passenger seat of her MINI Cooper with her cheek pressed against the window—the cool glass soothing her jagged nerves. Headlights reflected in the side mirror. For the second night in a row, her boss was acting as an escort for her.

"I hate Evan had to follow us to the ranch."

"You know he wouldn't have it any other way." Ridge slowed as the ranch came into view. "He takes his responsibilities seriously, especially when it comes to his employees."

She sat up straighter and glanced at the clock on the dash display. "It's midnight. And coming all the way out here is thirty minutes out of his way."

"I know you don't like feeling indebted to anyone, but can't you simply accept the fact that people who care about you will go above the call of duty to help when you're in need?" Ridge turned into the long driveway.

Jane twisted in her seat and watched as Evan stopped at the edge of the road. Ridge rolled down his window and entered the code for the gate. As soon as they drove through and it closed behind them, Evan sped off.

"I didn't mean to sound ungrateful," Jane said as she settled back in her seat.

"I know," Ridge replied. His tone held a hint of sadness.

Was he thinking about the summer before tenth grade? Her father had injured his back and had to miss three months of work, and because of a lack of funds, she'd had to drop out of the foreign exchange program just weeks before jetting off to Japan.

When Ridge had found out, he'd gone to his grandfather and asked him for the money. Then he showed up on the Masons' doorstep with an envelope full of cash. Desperate to keep her parents from hearing Ridge's offer, Jane had placed her hand on his chest and walked him backward onto the dark porch.

Then she accused him of trying to be a savior for his poor classmate, while he accused her of being silly and overreacting. She'd instantly replied that he wasn't a fairy godmother, and she wasn't Cinderella before slamming the door into the house behind her. She raced past her parents and Justin, and locked herself in her bedroom, where she lay on the bed crying for hours. The boy she'd recently developed romantic feelings for had seen her as nothing more than a charity case. It wasn't that her family had been poor. Her father had provided a good living for his wife and children, but a loss of income, even temporarily, required sacrifices. Jane never resented the fact that her plan to be an exchange student had fallen through. Such is life. Sometimes plans change.

Her face warmed as she recalled the interaction, and she pressed her cheek against the cool glass again. Her rejection of his offer to fund her trip hurt Ridge's feelings, and it took months to repair their damaged friendship. If it hadn't been for Justin, Jane wasn't sure she and Ridge ever would have gotten past the misunderstanding. Funny how Justin had been the one to heal their broken friendship and his death had been what tore it apart again.

Ridge drove past the main house, sitting in darkness on the hill overlooking the property just as it had the previous night. Had he told his mother that Jane was staying in the barn? Eleanor Snyder had always been so welcoming to Jane. She'd sent a letter of sympathy when Justin had passed and had even invited Jane and her mother to lunch many times in the years since. Although Jane had always strove to be respectful, she'd found an excuse not to attend each time. However, her mother always accepted the invitations.

As a result, unlike Jane and Ridge's relationship, Justin's death had drawn their mothers closer together, the two women forming a friendship that they'd never had while their children were growing up. Jane was thankful that Ridge's mom had made the effort to reach out to her mom. Cindy Mason had spent most of her life being a stay-at-home wife. Getting out of the house after losing her husband and son had been good for her. Now, she was involved in church and social activities, and she also worked part-time at the local library. Maybe Jane would find a moment to stop by the main house, say hello to Mrs. Snyder and let her know how much she appreciated the woman for befriending her mom.

Snap out of it, Jane. This isn't the time for a social visit. First up, finish grades. Next, you must enhance the photos to catch Aunt Nikki's killer before he kills you, too.

SIX

Holding a thermos of coffee in one hand and an insulated cooler in the other, Ridge climbed the stairs to the loft apartment. He hoped Jane was awake. It was only 7:55 a.m. He hadn't planned to check on her until nine o'clock, but he'd been awake since 4:30 a.m. When he'd been unable to go back to sleep, he'd swept and mopped every floor in his small house, then he'd worked in his garden, hoeing weeds as the sunrise lit the morning sky. What felt like eons later, but had only been ninety minutes, he'd taken a hot shower and got ready for the day. Then he set about to cook his breakfast, preparing scrambled eggs with cheese, sausage gravy and biscuits—making way more than he could eat himself. Which meant only one thing. He had to take the leftovers to Jane before they got too cold to eat.

The door of the apartment flew open as he reached the second-floor landing. Jane stood in the doorway—her face makeup free and her brown hair captured in a messy bun like she had always worn in school when they were studying for exams. His breath caught in his chest. She had always been a natural beauty with bright eyes and high cheekbones.

Her eyes widened at the sight of him. Blushing, she smoothed her hair and looked down. "I was just headed to my car to get my satchel. I didn't expect to run into anyone. I must look a fright."

Same old Jane. Why was it she never could see her own beauty? He blamed Tracey Drummond and all the other kids who taunted Jane with the nickname Plain Jane in seventh grade. Tracey had asked Ridge to be her date for homecoming. He'd politely refused, telling her he had already planned to attend with Jane and Justin. They had always attended all the football games together, with their team winning all of them. Even though Ridge had known there was no such thing as luck when it came to winning games, he didn't see any reason to chance a loss by changing his routine and who he attended the game with. Not to mention, he simply did not like Tracey. She was rather spoiled, and when things didn't go her way, she punished others around her. Hence, her sticking

Jane with a nickname because Ridge preferred Jane's company over hers.

He held out the insulated bag and thermos. "Take these. I'll go grab the satchel out of your vehicle."

Jane eyed the offering. "What is all of this?"

"Breakfast. And coffee." He pressed the items into her hands, then turned and jogged down the stairs, thankful for the escape. Why was he having thoughts of wanting to defend Jane's beauty to all their seventh-grade classmates? They were all grown adults now, living productive lives and making the world a better place. Last he'd heard, Tracey was a lawyer who offered pro bono services for women in domestic abuse situations.

Stepping out into the cool morning air, he inhaled deeply and released slowly. The thoughts of Tracey and the hurt she'd caused Jane had brought up long squashed emotions inside him. The past is the past and no matter how much one wished to change it, it could not be erased or blotted out as if it never existed. But Ridge would give anything if he could replace the core memory that had caused Jane to withdraw into a shell, hiding behind an invisible shield.

If he recalled correctly, that had been about the same time Jane discovered her love of photography. Any time there was a group photo opportunity, she had grabbed the camera and offered to take the photos. Ridge hadn't been fooled by her hobby. He knew it had been an opportunity for Jane to hide. How could he help Jane realize there was nothing plain or ordinary about her? She was a thousand times more beautiful than any woman he'd ever met. More beautiful than any photograph ever taken.

After he grabbed Jane's satchel out of the back seat of the MINI Cooper, he reentered the barn and took the stairs two at a time. The door to the apartment was open, so he rapped his knuckles on the exterior wall and walked in.

Jane sat at the small round table, a plate of food and a cup of the steaming coffee in front of her. "Thank you for breakfast."

"You're welcome." He hooked the satchel on her chair.

Grabbing a mug out of the cabinet, Ridge picked up the vacuum flask and poured himself a cup of coffee. Then he settled into the seat beside her. "How did you sleep?"

"Except for setting an alarm to wake up every hour from midnight until three, I slept fine."

"Your O2 levels were good?"

She took a sip of coffee. "Um…yes. After four consistently high readings, I skipped the remaining hourly checks, which allowed me four and a half hours of uninterrupted sleep."

She'd only just woken at 7:30 a.m.? "I'm sorry. I should have texted you before I dropped by."

"Why?" she asked. "This barn and apartment belong to your family. I'm just a temporary guest."

"You used to be more than that," he replied softly. "At one point you were like part of the family. I've missed you. And Justin."

A muscle in her jaw twitched, as if she were literally biting her tongue. Her silence was worse than suffering a thousand paper cuts. If only she would yell at him. Tell him what a horrible person he was. Never once had she said anything to him directly about Justin's death. At the funeral, she'd stared at him blankly, crossing her arms over her stomach, as a not-so-subtle barrier between them, when he'd attempted to hug her.

Mrs. Mason, ever the epitome of a gracious woman, had pulled Ridge into a warm hug and thanked him for being Justin's friend and honorary brother. Silent tears had racked his body. When he'd stepped out of Justin's grieving mother's arms, Jane had been nowhere in sight. After the service, while heading to his vehicle, Ridge overheard Jane tell Carolina she would never forgive him for Justin's death.

You didn't lose just one of your best friends on that battlefield, Snyder. You lost both of them. And it's best if you never forget it. Pro-tect Jane from the killer and then walk away. Let her live her life in peace. You don't deserve anything more.

Entering the last grade into the software program, Jane saved her work and logged out. Then she stood and stretched. She had been sitting hunched over for most of the day. First, sitting at the small dinette table grading papers. Then, after a brief lunch break, she'd spent the past two hours double-checking averages for every student in each class and entering the grades into the college's database.

What time was it? She glanced at her smart-watch. It was 2:53 p.m. She had exactly seven minutes to get changed for her meeting with Summer Fisher. Jane had promised Summer they would meet to discuss her grades at the end of the semester and make plans for her path forward. Thankfully, the strategies that Summer had implemented since her diagnosis seemed to be helping and she had gone from failing most of her classes to passing all of them. That didn't mean Jane could go back on her promise to be there for her student. After struggling through grades K–12 and not feeling like she had anyone on her side, it had taken a lot to get Summer to trust that Jane truly cared about her success in school and would be her advocate.

Ridge's reaction that morning when Jane had mentioned her need to keep the appointment with her student had been predictable, but thankfully she had persuaded him to drive her to the campus. Of course, it had taken her calling campus security—securing permission to park in the visitor parking in front of the building and arranging for an escort for them to and from her office—and her promise they would spend no more than thirty minutes on campus. She appreciated his concern and his dedication to protect her, but after two attacks on campus, did he really think she'd want to spend more time there than was absolutely necessary? If she didn't think it would set Summer back psychologically, Jane would email her and ask to reschedule their meeting. She couldn't betray the trust they had worked so hard to build. Also, completing this task would finish her semester commitments, allowing her to focus on the photographs of Aunt Nikki's and Phoebe's murders. Photographs the killer obviously thought held clues that would point to him.

Crossing to the small bedroom area, Jane quickly changed into a pair of jeans and a Blackberry Falls Community College T-shirt. Then she slipped her feet into her sneakers and quickly tied them. Normally, she wouldn't dress so casually to meet with a student, but she had a limited wardrobe with her. Besides, this was a brief meeting, and she wasn't likely to run into any of her colleagues.

Knock. Knock. Knock. "Jane, are you ready to go?" Ridge asked.

"Coming!" She jogged to the door and opened it. Her breath caught in her chest. As much as Jane would like to blame her sudden inability to breathe on the small amount of exertion she'd used to cross the tiny living space, she knew the tightness in her chest was caused by the sight of the man standing before her.

Freshly shaven and dressed in dark jeans and a white button-down shirt, the sleeves cuffed and pushed up on his muscular forearms, he looked more like a man picking up a date than a former friend acting as a bodyguard.

"Ready?" he asked, one eyebrow raised.

"Uh, um…yes." She grabbed her slender cross-body purse off the entryway table and followed him down the stairs. "Thank you for agreeing to take me to my meeting."

He opened the door that led outside and held it for her. "Just remember, you promised the meeting would be brief, and I'm staying as close to you as possible."

"Understood." Jane stepped outside into the

bright sunlight and immediately shaded her eyes. Determined to finish all her grading so she could devote her full attention to solving her aunt's cold-case murder, she hadn't so much as looked out a window all day. The birds were chirping and the smell of freshly mowed grass filled her senses.

She glanced around. The snowcapped mountains in the distance stood in stark contrast to the green fields dotted with wildflowers, and she suddenly realized what a beautiful day it truly was.

How could so much evil exist in a world with such abundant beauty? Despite the warm temperatures, a shiver raced along Jane's spine, causing her body to tremble.

Ridge draped an arm across her shoulders and pulled her to his side. "Are you okay?"

"I'm fine." She gave herself a mental shake and looked up, meeting his eyes. It had been a long time since they'd walked side by side like this with his arm around her. Ridge stood a full foot taller than Jane's five feet two inches. When they were in high school and she'd go watch him play baseball, he'd always liked to tease her about fitting under his arms and she'd always push him away playfully, telling him to get his sweaty armpits away from her. Only, this time, he wasn't sweaty at all. Hints of bergamot and cedarwood wafted around her. A more subtle scent than the body spray he'd used as a teenager.

Her heart fluttered, and for the second time since he'd arrived at her door, her breath caught in her chest. Taking one sidestep, she moved away from him, his arm dropping to his side. "I see you got your truck back," she observed as they rounded the corner of the barn—his big truck overshadowed her smaller car.

"Yeah. Evan said they had finished with it, so I had Wyatt drive me to pick it up at lunchtime." Ridge opened the passenger-side door. "As much as I've enjoyed riding around in your MINI, I thought we'd take my truck this time."

"Did they find any clues to the man's identity?" she asked as she climbed inside, though she knew if they had, he would have mentioned it before now.

"No." Closing her door, he jogged around the front of the vehicle and slid into the driver's seat as she clicked her seat belt into place.

Soon they were driving down the back roads toward Blackberry Falls, the windows down and Ridge's favorite country music playing on the radio. If it weren't for the current situation Jane found herself in, she could almost pretend they were once again high school seniors headed to a football game. Only, if that were the case, Justin would be in the back seat complaining about the music and pleading with Ridge to change the station to one that played rock 'n' roll.

Tears stung the backs of her eyes. Oh, what she'd give to have one more day with Justin. She'd happily listen to the music of his choice without complaint, and she wouldn't even protest eating pineapple on pizza while they watched a horror movie.

"Are you going to answer that?" Ridge asked, pulling her from her thoughts.

"What?" Jane furrowed her brow.

"Your phone." He glanced at her purse, laying at her feet on the floorboard. "It's ringing."

"Oh," she exclaimed as the ringtone she'd set specifically for her boss penetrated her brain. "That's Evan."

The ringing had stopped by the time she dug the phone out of her purse, but before she could dial him back, it started again. "Must be urgent." She slid her finger across the screen and lifted the phone to her ear. "Hi, boss. Sorry, I—"

"Where are you?" Evan demanded, cutting off her apology.

His behavior was totally out of character. "I'm headed to campus with Ridge. I have a meeting with a student."

"Reschedule the meeting. I need you at Riverchase ASAP." Riverchase was an assisted living facility near a lake a few miles out of town.

"Can it wait until after my meeting? It won't last long."

"No. There's been a murder. I need crime scene photos." Evan cleared his throat. "And Jane, I may be mistaken, but I suspect this is related to your aunt's case. I don't want to say more until you get here."

"We need to stop by my house and pick up my equipment," Jane said as she tightened her grip on the phone and met Ridge's gaze.

Without questioning, Ridge executed a U-turn and sped toward her brick rancher they'd passed a few miles back.

"We'll be there in fifteen minutes," Jane said into the phone. Then she disconnected the call and quickly sent a message to Summer, canceling their meeting and promising to reschedule soon.

Ridge pulled into her driveway and parked. "What's going on?"

"We need to get to Riverchase, the assisted living community. There's been a murder. I have to take photos, but also, Evan thinks this murder has something to do with my Aunt Nikki's murder."

"Well then, let's get your gear loaded and head that way."

Jane didn't have to be told twice. She was out of the vehicle and unlocking her front door by the time Ridge made it to the porch steps.

Lord, I'm sorry someone has been killed, but if this death is related to Aunt Nikki's murder, I pray we find the connection and that it leads us to the murderer. For someone who hadn't prayed much in the past four years, she was getting very comfortable talking to the Lord. Strangely, it seemed to give her a sense of peace. She'd have to examine what that meant after they solved the cold case. But in the meantime, she wouldn't worry about what was triggering her need to pray. Instead, she'd embrace it as a means of talking through her desires, as one might do talking to their best friend. The way she once had shared all her hopes and dreams with Ridge. But unlike her relationship with God, she knew no amount of talking would mend the rift between her and the man acting as her bodyguard.

SEVEN

Ridge stood off to one side of the crime scene, watching Jane work. He wasn't sure what had happened once she received the phone call from Evan, but after picking up her photography equipment, she'd remained silent for the drive to the retirement community. Maybe he was reading too much into it. She could have just been preparing herself to do her job. The instant they'd arrived at the scene, she'd been hyper-focused, listening to Evan's commands as she snapped pictures from every angle.

Someone had strangled retired Blackberry Falls police officer Gordon Davidson with his laptop computer cord while he sat in his wheelchair in his sunroom. He lived in the assisted living area of the retirement community, his home a one-bedroom cottage at the edge of the property near the lake. The housekeeper, who cleaned each assisted living cottage twice weekly, discovered his body. The state of his body suggested he had been dead for at least twenty-four hours, if not longer, although they would have to wait for the autopsy to confirm this.

Evan crossed over to Ridge and leaned against the wall next to him. "She's very good at her job."

"I can tell." Ridge turned to the police chief. "What do you think happened here? Murders in Blackberry Falls are rare, and I'd suspect murders of senior citizens in assisted living facilities are even more so."

"Most definitely not a common occurrence." Evan frowned, his brow creasing as a pensive look crossed his eyes.

Ridge followed Evan's gaze. Jane had finished taking pictures and was in the process of packing up her equipment. Squaring his shoulders, Ridge turned back to the police chief. "What are you not telling me?"

A muscle twitched in Evan's jaw. After several seconds, he replied, "I believe this murder is connected to the Brush Hollow Reservoir Murders."

"What makes you think that?" Ridge asked.

"I'd like to know, too." Jane walked up to them, her camera bag in hand.

Evan motioned them to follow him into the living room, away from the crime scene technician collecting fingerprints and other evidence in the sunroom. "Gordon was the detective in charge of the original investigation," he supplied once they were out of earshot. He met Jane's eyes. "Not solving the case always haunted him."

"If he couldn't solve the case, why would the killer murder him now?" she asked Evan.

"I'm not sure. But we discovered a journal full of notes on the case tucked underneath Gordon. The cushion he sat on in the wheelchair was pushed aside and bunched up in the middle, as if he'd been in a hurry to conceal the journal."

"You think he was going through the notes to assist with the new investigation?" Ridge asked. "And that got him killed?"

"Gordon was a respected member of the police force and the community. A man with no known enemies. Seems coincidental that someone would kill him now, just when we're reopening the case he worked so hard to solve. Besides, I don't believe in coincidences."

Neither did Ridge. If what Evan said was true, that meant the killer would take out anyone he thought might have the slightest chance of exposing his identity. Which wasn't really shocking. "Do you think Gordon knew his killer?"

"There weren't any signs of forced entry that I could tell while taking photos," Jane supplied.

"Footprints indicate the killer came onto and exited the property through the woods bordering the lake." Evan turned to Jane. "You got shots of the prints, right?"

"Of course," Jane acknowledged. "But Officer Benson wouldn't let me go into the woods. He said you'd given orders. I was to stay within sight of the cottage and within sight of at least one member of the team at all times."

Evan tipped his head. "I followed the prints through the woods to the road. I'm pretty sure the killer is long gone, as I didn't see any signs of him, but we can't be too cautious."

Jane shuddered ever so slightly, and Ridge had to ball his fist to keep from putting his arm around her. He couldn't keep offering comfort the way he had when they were friends. He had to keep things professional.

"The muddy footprints on the back deck show he came in through the sunroom," Evan continued. "The housekeeper verified that Gordon normally kept his doors locked, unless he was sitting out on the deck. Which, according to her, he only did in the early morning hours before it became too hot. Time of death will tell us more, but that gives us two scenarios. One, Gordon was sitting on the deck, the killer came up, followed him inside and killed him. Two, Gordon was in the sunroom going over his notes when the killer knocked on the sunroom door, and Gordon let him inside."

"What does your gut tell you?" Ridge pressed. One of the first lessons he'd learned as a SEAL had been to trust his gut. The one time he second-guessed himself, he lost a third of his platoon, including Justin.

"I try to keep my gut feelings to myself," Evan replied. "Until I have evidence to support them."

"But…you have suspicions, right?" Jane pressed.

Evan crossed to the windows that faced the back of the property. "I think it's most likely Gordon saw his killer coming out of the woods. He would have known if he could see the person walking toward him, they could see him, too. Not having time to hide his journal, he tucked it under his body. Then he opened the door and let the killer inside."

"Do you think he knew the person was coming to kill him?" Jane whispered.

"No way to tell," Evan replied. "If he didn't know it before he let the man inside, I'm sure he knew it soon thereafter."

The coroner walked over to Evan. "Chief, they're getting ready to transport the body to the morgue, and I'm on my way to Gordon's daughter's house to notify her of his death. I wondered if you wanted to accompany me?"

"Okay. I'll follow you." Evan turned to Ridge. "Get her home safely. I don't have an officer I can send to follow you, so you're on your own."

"Don't worry. I won't let anything happen to her." And Ridge meant every word.

The only way the Brush Hollow Reservoir Killer would get to Jane would be if Ridge were dead first. He reached for the bulky camera bag. After a slight hesitation, Jane relinquished it to him. They followed Evan out of the house, parting ways in the driveway.

Dear heavenly Father, I pray you will watch over us and protect us as we travel back to the ranch. Please, give me the foresight to detect any dangers along the way and the strength to ward them off. In Christ's most holy name, Amen.

Jane closed her eyes and rested her head against the back of the truck seat. Deep down in her heart she knew she wasn't responsible for Gordon Davidson's death, but that knowledge hadn't stopped a weight of guilt from settling in her heart. If she hadn't gone to Evan and insisted that Aunt Nikki's murder be the next cold case they looked into, Gordon would still be alive, sitting in his sunroom, carving small figurines.

"If I offered you a dollar, would you share with me?"

"What?" She swiveled her head and opened her eyes. Sitting in the driver's seat of his pickup truck, he looked masculine and in control. Which, if she were completely fair in her assessment, was the same way he'd looked driving her compact MINI Cooper. Why did he have to look so handsome?

"The old saying is a penny for your thoughts. Even with your eyes closed, you looked so deep in thought, I didn't think a penny would be a fair value for your thoughts." Ridge smiled at her and offered her a one-shoulder shrug.

Her heart did a fluttery little dance. She sat up straight and forced herself to take a couple of slow breaths. "I was just thinking about the very real possibility that Gordon Davidson's death could have been prevented if I hadn't asked to look into the Brush Hollow murders."

"Don't let your mind go there. It's a dangerous line of thought." His face paled and his grip tightened on the steering wheel. "You don't know that the events that led to Gordon's murder had anything to do with you. The killer may have had another reason for killing him. But even if, as you say, his murder was a direct result of the case being reopened, it's not on you. You didn't cause his death and you couldn't stop it."

She bit the corner of her lower lip. Had Ridge used a similar speech to appease his own guilt over her brother's death? Was Justin's death really Ridge's fault? Had Jane been wrong to blame him all these years?

Even though Jane and her mom had both tried to persuade Justin to go to community college and wait a couple of years before enlisting, he hadn't listened. He'd told them the military believed eighteen was old enough to make his own choices, even life-changing ones, and he didn't need anyone else's permission. Even though he'd never talked about joining any branch of the military, Jane couldn't say with certainty that he wouldn't have joined even if it hadn't been for Ridge. Justin had never had a plan for his life. Throughout school, he had been the kid that only did what was required to get through his classes, nothing more. Content and happy to make average grades.

No. Ridge was the one who convinced Justin he needed to make something out of his life and told him the Navy would make a man out of him. Well, it had made a man out of him and then it had taken his life and future away before it even had much of a chance to get started.

These two situations were not the same. She hadn't been the one to talk Gordon into looking into Nikki's cold-case murder. He'd done it all on his own, knowing that doing so could be dangerous. As a seventy-year-old retired police officer, he'd lived long enough to know the risks of his actions.

"I guess you're right. Gordon could have already been looking into the case even before the news got out that Evan and I were taking a second look at the crime scene photos. If it's the only case in his career that he wasn't able to solve, I imagine it would have been on his mind that he wanted it solved before he died. And he was in frail health." She lay back and closed her eyes again, praying the action would end any further conversation. "Wake me when we get to the ranch."

"Once we get back to the ranch, I think it's a good idea if you lie low for a few days, don't go out in public," Ridge said, obviously not taking the hint.

"Um, 'kay," she replied.

"Do you need anything before we leave town? We could stop quickly at the grocery store or if you need more clothes or anything."

"Uh-huh," she murmured, half-listening.

"Could you focus? Just for a moment?" he asked sternly.

"What?" she said, more harshly than intended. Releasing an exasperated sigh, Jane pushed upright in the seat.

In the soft light of the interior of the pickup cab, she saw his jaw tighten. For as long as she'd known him, he'd always clenched his jaw when he was trying to keep from saying something that he thought would hurt the other person's feelings. What had he asked? Did she need anything from the store before they left town? Shame washed over her. He may have offered to protect her from the Brush Hollow murderer, but he hadn't asked for this. Whether he'd played a role in Justin's death or not, he didn't deserve her rudeness. Not after all he'd done for her the past few days.

"I'm sorry. I shouldn't have snapped," Jane whispered.

"It's my fault. I shouldn't have pushed," he replied.

Is this what they'd become? People who couldn't talk honestly to each other? Who tiptoed around each other's feelings? Jane scrutinized Ridge's features. A mask had fallen into place, his gaze fixed on the road ahead.

"There is no excuse for my rudeness." Fighting the urge to fidget, she clasped her hands in her lap. "I should have warned you I wouldn't be talkative on the ride back to the ranch. It takes me a while to decompress after visiting a crime scene. Photographing any scene can be challenging, but murder scenes are extra hard. The things I see and the sheer amount of time it takes to get every photo just right, praying I don't miss anything important..."

"I should have realized that's what was going on. I've been there. Not as a photographer, but I've seen my fair share of death..."

For the first time since they'd reconnected, she realized the boy she'd grown up with had been replaced by a man who had seen far worse than anything she'd ever experienced. He'd witnessed death as it occurred, while trying to stay alive himself. How many men had died in the ambush that had killed her brother? Five? Military brothers and friends, dying in front of him. Had he attempted to save any of them? What had it been like? She'd thought many times about seeking Ridge out and asking him to tell her all the details about that day. What had gone wrong? Why couldn't he save Justin? What were her brother's last words?

People often talk about the connection twins share. How they feel each other's pain, even if they are thousands of miles apart. But she had felt nothing unusual the day Justin died. Not one hint of something horrible happening to her twin on the other side of the world. She'd been on a date with Barry. He'd flown in to celebrate the two-year anniversary of the day they'd met. They'd had an early dinner, and then they'd strolled through the Denver Botanic Gardens afterward.

Her heart rate accelerated as she recalled the night that the man she had loved had attempted to propose to her. As they walked, Barry had listed all the things he loved about her. Midway through the proposal, her phone rang. It was her mother's ringtone. He'd asked her to ignore it, and she'd complied, initially. But each time the ringing stopped, it started again within seconds. That had been her first clue that something devastating had happened. She'd answered the phone despite the scowl marring Barry's face. And her world had fallen apart.

Her brother was dead. Mom was inconsolable. And Barry was livid that Jane had messed up his perfectly orchestrated proposal. She'd known then that she would never wear Barry's ring. A man who put more emphasis on a proposal than he did on family wasn't someone she wanted in her life. Without ever knowing it, Justin had done what he'd always done as her big brother. He'd protected her from making the mistake of a lifetime.

EIGHT

Zzzz. A gentle snore sounded from the passenger seat. Silence had descended on the vehicle before they'd even cleared the city limits headed to the lesser populated farm and ranch land out in the county. Ridge had wanted to push Jane to talk through her feelings, knowing she was blaming herself for Gordon Davidson's murder. But doing so would have only backfired and most likely caused her to clam up even more. Or at least that had been his experience in high school any time he'd pushed for her to express her feelings.

His mom had mentioned wanting to visit with Jane while she was staying on the ranch. Maybe he'd see if Mom could drop by the barn apartment and check on Jane tomorrow. Mom and Jane had always had a good relationship until Justin's death when Jane distanced herself from anyone connected to Ridge. He prayed once this ordeal was over Jane could find it in her heart to forgive him for not being able to save Justin.

They neared the narrow two-lane bridge that crossed a section of the Arkansas River. Three more miles and they'd be home. The tension in his muscles eased. He'd spent the entire drive looking in his rearview mirror for any signs the killer was following them. Thankfully, the drive had been quiet. There had been no vehicles following behind him, and he had only passed two cars along the way, which wasn't unusual for ten o'clock on a Wednesday evening.

Slowing his speed to soften the normal jolt that occurred when entering the bridge from this side, he eased onto the concrete platform, his truck lights shining on the plywood and tin patching the railing where a feed truck had crashed six months earlier. The bridge connected the people who lived in this area to the rest of the county. The county road commissioner had promised to complete the repairs in a timely manner, but Ridge had learned long ago, for government entities, the concept of time varied widely.

He was halfway across the bridge when a large black SUV approached from the opposite side. Instead of waiting his turn—like most residents had done since the bridge became damaged—the driver entered the bridge and raced toward them. If Ridge hadn't already passed the halfway point, he would have been tempted to back off the bridge. At this point, his best option was to continue forward and pass the other driver quickly. Whatever the other person's hurry, Ridge was thankful they were being respectful and staying close to the undamaged guardrail on their side, allowing Ridge to continue to hug the middle line. However, as the other vehicle drew near, it inched closer to Ridge's truck. From that point onward, everything seemed to happen quickly and in slow motion at the same time.

The SUV veered into Ridge's lane, and he moved a few inches to the right as he pressed down on the horn. What was the guy thinking? Jane jerked awake with a gasp. Ridge caught sight of the driver, who wore a black hoodie and a white ghost mask. Adrenaline coursed through Ridge's veins as he tightened his grip on the steering wheel.

"Hang on!" he ordered Jane.

She grasped the grab handle above the door and braced her other hand on the console between their seats. Ridge spun the wheel to the left as the SUV rammed into his truck. Metal scraped against metal. He fought to maintain control, pressing down on the gas, desperate to gain traction as the masked man in the full-size SUV worked to push the truck closer to the temporary railing—one that Ridge doubted would prevent his king cab pickup truck from going over the edge.

"He's going to push us into the water!" Jane exclaimed as the other driver forced Ridge's truck sideways.

Ridge wished he could offer her reassurance, but if he couldn't gain traction, that was exactly what the outcome would be. "Brace yourself," he ordered.

His tires squalled and the smell of melting rubber wafted through the air vents. The front passenger side of his truck connected with the plywood and the sound of splintering wood registered seconds before his front tires dangled off the bridge. The SUV stopped, backed up a couple of feet and charged them, the front end connecting with the bumper of the truck, sending Ridge's vehicle into a somersault in open air.

Jane's piercing scream filled the cab.

Ridge thrust his right arm across her chest. *Lord, please protect us!*

The truck completed a complete rotation, then sliced into the water at a slight angle— front-end first—with a jolt. The seat belt tightened on Ridge's chest as cold water seeped into the cab. Thankfully, the angle of the impact had kept the airbags from deploying. However, because they'd had above average rainfall the previous two months, the water levels of the river were higher than normal, creating a stronger than usual current in the river that was pushing his truck downstream as it filled with water.

Ridge released a breath and unfastened his seat belt. Free from his restraint, he turned to Jane. "Are you hurt?"

"I'm stuck! I can't get free." She fumbled with her seat belt, her movements jerky and her body trembling. He'd seen the same thing happen to soldiers in combat after a traumatic experience. She was going into shock.

Ridge reached across and depressed the lever, releasing her. The instant she was free, she dove into his arms. Pulling her close, he clutched her tightly.

"What do we do? How do we get out?" Her breath brushed his neck as she spoke.

He eased her away from him, sweeping her hair off her face and out of her eyes. "We need to go out the window. But the current is strong, and we have to be careful not to be pulled under the truck."

Her eyes widened, and she shook her head vehemently. "I can't do that."

She had always been afraid of water and had refused to take swimming lessons with him and Justin. Ridge would have to carry her on his back.

"You don't have to swim. I will get you to safety."

The hood of the truck dipped farther into the lake. The water level rose inside the cab. No time to waste.

Pressing the button to roll down the driver's side window, he turned back to Jane. "I'll climb through the window first, then I want you to follow me. Once you get out, you'll put your arms around my neck, and I'll get us to shore."

Her eyes doubled in size—fear reflected inside them. "No. I'll weigh you down. We'll both drown. You swim to safety and get help. I'll wait here."

Ridge took in her petite frame. He had swum in much more difficult conditions, carrying a lot more weight. But even if that wasn't the case, there was no way he was leaving her behind. "The current is carrying the truck downstream. As it moves, it will continue to fill with water. And it will sink fast. We probably have less than ninety seconds to get out and away from the vehicle."

He cupped her face between his hands and looked deep into her blue eyes—the same color Justin's had been. Ridge had watched the light leave Justin's eyes as his life drained from his body. He would not allow the same thing to happen with Jane. If she died, he would, too. He would not leave her.

Whether from the chill of the water or the fear of dying, he did not know, a desperate need to prove to them both that they were alive and would survive drew him to her. He lowered his head, and his lips claimed hers in a kiss that held an urgency he'd never felt before.

Water splashed his bare waist. Pulling back, he looked down. The water level had risen another foot. They were out of time.

"Be ready to go, on my command," he ordered, his tone leaving no room for argument.

Jane nodded, wordlessly.

Ridge grasped the doorframe and squeezed through the window opening. Keeping a firm grip on the vehicle, he held out a hand to Jane. "Now."

She put her hand in his and climbed over the center console. As Jane reached the driver's seat, the truck shifted and the top of the cab plunged below the water, causing Ridge to lose his hold on her.

"No! Dear Lord, please, don't let me lose her!" Ridge cried into the night.

Jane inhaled sharply, seconds before the water rose above her head. Holding her breath, she closed her eyes. *Lord, please let me wake up from this nightmare.* Only it wasn't a dream. It was real, and she was about to die. The truck connected with the bottom of the lake with a jolt.

Dear Lord, I am sorry I turned my back on You in my grief over losing Justin. Please forgive me. I know his death wasn't Your fault. It's not Ridge's fault, either. I pray Ridge doesn't blame himself for my death. It's not his fault I never learned to swim or that my panic cost us valuable time in exiting the vehicle. Please, Lord, take me quickly.

An unexplainable peace settled over her. She opened her eyes and slowly expelled air from her lungs, creating bubbles. She watched as they floated out the open window. Drawn to the bubbles, she pushed her upper body through the opening and released more air, watching the bubbles float upward. Suddenly, she didn't want to die without a fight. She had too much to live for. Her mother needed her. And she still needed to solve Aunt Nikki's murder.

To no avail, she kicked her feet and flailed her arms, fighting to follow the bubbles to the surface. *Please, Lord, save me.* She closed her eyes and tried to remember what she'd heard the instructor tell Justin and Ridge when they'd taken swim lessons. Push off the bottom, arms at your side, and kick to generate an upward motion.

Sinking to the riverbed, she bent her knees and pushed upward, kicking with all her might. It wasn't working! Just as she was about to give up, Ridge swam toward her. She gasped, inhaling water. Tears stung her eyes. He looped his left arm around her chest, and suddenly she was being lifted upward. They broke through the surface of the water and she coughed, gasping for air.

"It's okay. You're safe," he assured her. "Hold onto me and kick your feet… Not too hard."

Coughing deeply and expelling water, she wrapped her arms around his neck and did as he instructed. If she survived this, she would sign up for swim lessons immediately. She never wanted to be in this situation again.

"The current is too strong. We'll never make it to shore." Jane didn't even try to hide the panic in her voice. What would be the point? Other than Justin, Ridge knew her better than anyone—her fears included.

The swirling water pushed them farther downstream, and she tightened her hold on Ridge. He twisted his neck. "Not so tight."

Lacing her fingers together, she loosened her grip and met his gaze. "Sorry."

"I've swum in far worse conditions." He

broke eye contact and looked around. Then he jerked his head toward the right bank. "We're closer to this side. It'll be best if you roll onto your back and float as I swim us to shore."

Fear wrapped around her chest and gripped her like a vise clamp, sucking the air out of her lungs. The one time she'd agreed to let her mom teach her to float on her back, she'd sank like a rock, swallowed a lot of water, and refused to go near a pool again.

"Trust me," Ridge whispered, as if he could read her mind.

Lord, keep my nerves at bay. Calm my anxiety. Give me the courage I need to do what I need to do so Ridge can save us.

She took a couple of deep breaths, and then she rolled onto her back. The water whipped around her, filling her ears and splashing her face. She closed her eyes and focused on her breathing while counting backward from one hundred, something her grandmother had taught her to do when she felt anxious and needed to calm her mind. Ridge slid his arm so it wrapped around her upper chest and his hand gripped her under her arm. Jane grasped his bicep with both her hands. If he lost his hold on her, she would fight to maintain her hold on him. Because if they got separated, she would drown.

Seventy-two, seventy-one, seventy, sixty-nine, sixty—

"Okay. Stand up," Ridge said, breaking into her thoughts.

"What?" Water filled her mouth, causing her to sputter and gasp.

Ridge lifted her upward, planting her feet on the muddy bottom of the riverbed, the water hitting her mid-thigh, and pounded on her back with the palm of his hand. "Are you okay?"

"I'm fine." Turning away with a wave of her hand, she trudged through the water and collapsed on a boulder at the edge of the riverbank.

Ridge sank down on the rock beside her. She pushed upward, pulling her knees to her chest and wrapping her arms around them.

"Thank you for saving me."

"You're not safe yet. We still need to make it to the ranch." He looked toward the bridge. "And I have no clue where our attacker went."

Jane followed his gaze. Clouds had drifted in front of the moon, making it impossible to tell if the man in the SUV was sitting there with the headlights off. But she knew better than to think that the killer had left without knowing if they had lived or died. If he wasn't on the bridge, he was hiding somewhere nearby. Of that, she had no doubt.

* * *

A stiff wind blew across the water, ruffling Ridge's hair. Jane shivered and wrapped her arms around her body, reminding him she was a civilian. The conditions he'd been trained to endure were unfamiliar to her. He'd do well to remember that.

The most important thing at the moment was to get her to safety. Ridge had no way of knowing if she'd swallowed too much water while she'd been underwater. It was imperative that she be checked out by a doctor.

Was their attacker hiding in wait? A pair of night vision goggles sure would come in handy. Too bad Ridge didn't carry around all the tactical gear that he'd once carried on his person as a navy SEAL in combat situations. He pursed his lips, and his jaw twitched. Since Ridge couldn't see the killer, he'd have to use his knowledge of the territory and instincts to guide them to the ranch.

He stood, turned and held his hand out to Jane. After a slight hesitation, she slipped her hand in his and allowed him to help her up off the boulder.

"What's the plan?" she asked, her voice raspy.

His chest tightened. He'd heard of instances where people died hours after water entered their lungs in a near-drowning situation. It was called second drowning. It was crucial to seek medical attention immediately.

It was a longshot, but just maybe his phone would work to make a call to 911. Silently berating himself for not calling the minute they got out of the river, Ridge reached in his back pocket. No. His phone was gone. The water must have swept away it.

"Do you have your phone?" he asked with little hope.

"No, it's in my purse in the—" Jane gasped. "My camera! It's at the bottom of the river." She took a couple of steps toward the river.

Ridge grabbed her arm, halting her. "You can't go back in there. You nearly drowned."

"We have to save my equipment." She fought to pull free of his grasp. "All the crime scene photos I took… Evidence to solve Gordon's murder—which might tell us who the killer is—could literally be floating downstream at this very moment…"

"You don't know how to swim," he reminded her.

She spun around and faced him. "You do, though." She grabbed his shirt in her fists. "You've got to go get it. Please."

"Sweetie, I can't." He guided her back to the rock, helped her to sit and knelt in front of her. "It's too dangerous to leave you here alone. Besides, your camera is probably already beyond repair…"

"No. No. No. Don't say that. The case is water-resistant. I bought a good one—to protect from rain and spills and such." Jane looked over his shoulder. "This is a little more water than I anticipated, though."

"Once we get somewhere safe, I'll—" He paused at the sound of a twig snapping in the woods to their right. Putting a finger to his lips, he helped Jane to stand and steered her into a cluster of trees. Hidden behind a large box elder tree, they watched silently.

Snap. Crack. Thud. Jane clutched his arm as more sounds came from the woods. The person after them obviously wasn't concerned with being discrete. Ridge prayed the man didn't have a gun. In hand-to-hand combat, Ridge did not doubt he'd come out the victor. But if there was a weapon, he'd have to stand down. Not because he was afraid, but because he could not risk Jane being struck by a stray bullet. *Crash.* Ridge's muscles tensed as a dark figure emerged from the woods. His breath caught in his chest as he watched a mountain lion—approximately eight feet long and weighing two hundred pounds—meander to the water's edge, dip his head and drink.

Acutely aware of Jane standing like a statue

by his side, Ridge did the only thing he could do in this situation. He prayed. *Dear Heavenly Father, I know You are with us and we are to fear no evil. But, please, I pray the beautiful creature that You created—the powerful predator standing before us now—will turn and disappear into the night without noticing our presence.*

Minutes ticked by slowly. Jane's grasp on Ridge's arm tightened. And the mountain lion continued to drink from the not-so-still waters. After what felt like a lifetime, the muscular animal raised his head. Then he looked in their direction.

Don't come this way. You were not the opponent I was expecting. Please, don't make me fight you. Though I will, if you insist, to protect the woman beside me. Almost as if he had heard Ridge's silent plea, the animal released a high-pitched whistle and bound into the woods the same way he'd appeared. Once the animal was out of sight, Ridge released a sigh of relief.

"That was…scary," Jane said, releasing his arm and leaning against the tree trunk.

"Too close for comfort," he admitted. "Hopefully, we won't run into any more dangerous animals. I had thought we might travel through the woods to the bridge and then make our way to the ranch, but I'm second-guessing that decision now."

"Yeah, I don't think I'm up for a hike in the woods in the dark after seeing that big cat."

For a large portion of Highway 50, the Arkansas River ran alongside the road. Unfortunately, the current had pushed them far enough downstream that they couldn't see the road from their current vantage point. If his internal sense of direction wasn't off too much, he was sure they weren't more than a half mile from a section of river that would put them closer to the road. It would be the easiest route that would avoid them having to follow the mountain lion into the woods.

"We'll go this way." He cupped her elbow and guided her along the riverbank. "When the river curves, we shouldn't be far from Highway 50."

"Do you think we'll be able to flag down a vehicle at this time of night?"

"I hope so. But the minute we see a vehicle, you need to hide and stay out of sight. At least until I'm sure it's safe."

"Agreed." She nodded. "One hundred percent."

They continued along in silence, Ridge's mind running through all the scenarios that could happen once they reached the open road.

This late at night, it was possible they wouldn't even encounter another vehicle. Which meant walking to the closest house, about two miles away, making it even longer before he could seek medical attention for Jane. *Don't let your mind go there*.

"What are you thinking?" Jane asked.

"Just trying to map out a plan, in case we can't hitch a ride."

"Oh, that's easy. We hike to Mr. and Mrs. Kendall's house."

Ridge smiled. The woman beside him still had a lot of the characteristics of the girl she used to be, but she wasn't truly the same. Younger Jane, who didn't have an ounce of athleticism in her body, would have complained about the prospect of walking fifty feet in wet clothing and soggy shoes, let alone two miles. This Jane had not even shed a tear about her near-drowning experience. Which was something he hoped to talk to her about once this ordeal was over. Not the fact that she hadn't cried, but the need for her to face her fears and learn to swim. If he hadn't been there to rescue her… A shudder racked his body.

He really needed to learn to control his thoughts a little better. The way he had when he'd been in the military—categorizing details so they didn't control him and make him ineffective or cause him to be careless. But then he'd slipped up, and he'd failed the men under his charge. In that one instance, Justin's life was over. Ridge would die trying before he failed Jane, too.

NINE

The clouds shifted, revealing a bright full moon that acted as a giant streetlamp lighting their path. As they rounded the bend in the river, the rocky embankment beside the road came into view. There appeared to be several crevices where someone could hide out of sight.

The sound of a vehicle reached Ridge's ears. He hurriedly guided Jane to the embankment, urging her into one of the gaps. "Stay out of sight while I assess the situation. Do not come out, no matter what, unless I give the okay."

She wrapped her arms around her stomach, as if she were trying to hold herself together, and nodded.

Ridge quickly scaled the embankment. The pickup truck was approaching from the direction of the bridge. He couldn't tell the make or model. It was definitely not the SUV that had run them off the bridge. But he would not let his guard down until he knew Jane was safe.

The killer might have someone working with him. Or he could have carjacked the owner of the truck.

The truck slowed, pulling off the road onto the gravel shoulder. Temporarily blinded by the headlights, Ridge lifted a hand, shielding his eyes as he stepped to the side. Recognition was instant, and relief flooded his body.

"I've been searching for you," Wyatt declared as he stepped out of the vehicle. "Evan called when he couldn't reach you. He said you headed home with Jane hours ago. What happened to the bridge? Are you okay?" He paused and looked around. "Where is Jane?"

"I'll get her," Ridge replied. "But first, did you bring a gun?"

Wyatt frowned. "I have my rifle. Why?"

"The killer attacked us. Don't know where he went after he forced my truck off the bridge. Stand guard while I get Jane." Ridge turned and picked his way back down the rocky embankment, stopping short when he saw Jane on her way up. "I thought I told you to wait until I gave the all clear."

"I heard Wyatt. You Snyder boys are anything but quiet," she offered as an explanation as she drew closer. "I figured it was safe to come out. I'm wet and cold and ready to get someplace dry."

"Fair enough." He wrapped his hand around hers and helped her over a large rock.

When they reached the top of the embankment, Wyatt was waiting on them, rifle in hand. Ridge hurried Jane to the back door of the vehicle and opened it for her. After she had slid inside, he closed the door and turned to his brother. "We need to take her to the hospital. She swallowed a lot of water."

"I'm fine," Jane said loudly from the back seat. "Can't we just go to the ranch?"

"No, you—"

"Look," Wyatt interrupted Ridge, "let's discuss this in the vehicle."

He pursed his lips and nodded. Ridge hated to admit it but his brother was right. Every second they sat on the side of the road, the greater the risk the killer would return and find them. He knew better. It was dangerous for him to let his desire to look after Jane override his training. He had to stay on guard at all times.

"Since I'm riding shotgun, I might as well be in control of the rifle," Ridge said and held out his hand.

Wyatt handed over the weapon and slid behind the steering wheel, closing his door with a thud. Ridge jogged around the front of the vehicle and settled into the front passenger seat, quickly clicking his seat belt into place as he felt Jane's eyes boring into the back of his skull.

"I really think," Ridge began, softly, keeping his eyes forward, "you should be examined at the hospital. But I respect your right to make your own decision."

"Thank you," Jane replied. "Wyatt, would you, please, take me to the ranch? And, if it wouldn't be too much trouble, would you mind stopping at my house long enough for me to get more dry clothes?"

Wyatt chuckled under his breath. "Yes, ma'am." He shifted into Drive and executed a U-turn.

They neared the bridge and Ridge's gut tightened at the sight of the gaping hole in the guardrail. He turned to Wyatt. "May I use your phone?"

"Sure." Wyatt pointed to the glove compartment. "It's in there."

Ridge pulled it out and punched in Evan's number.

"Wyatt, did you find them?"

"He did," Ridge replied. "Sorry. I lost my phone at the bottom of the Arkansas River."

"What happened?"

"The killer forced my truck off the bridge." He sighed. "The *temporary fix* the county road department put up didn't hold. Anyway, my truck is at the bottom of the river, but Jane and I are safe."

"Tell him about my camera," Jane instructed.

Ridge pulled the phone away from his ear and pressed the speaker icon on the screen. "Evan, I have you on speaker now so Jane can join in the conversation."

"My camera bag is at the bottom of the river," Jane declared before her boss could speak. "We need divers out here to retrieve it."

"I'm a little more concerned with your well-being than I am your camera," Evan chided. "Are you hurt?"

"No. Ridge saved me before I swallowed much water."

"Are you still in the area of the bridge?" Evan asked. "I'll get an ambulance en route."

"We don't need an ambulance," she insisted. "We need divers. The camera has pictures on it that might lead us to the person doing all of this."

"We're headed to the ranch," Ridge replied. "After a quick stop at Jane's house so she can get more clothes."

"Okay, I'll meet you at the ranch and take your statements about the incident."

"What about my camera?"

"I'll have a dive team on the river at sunup."

"But—"

"I've made my decision," Evan said firmly. "It will be easier in the daylight. Be careful getting back to the ranch. I'll meet you there soon."

Evan disconnected the call, and Jane slumped against her seat, a scowl on her face. Ridge could almost read her mind. She'd always been impatient. Someone who wanted things done right then. She looked at life through lenses that only saw things as right or wrong. No gray areas in between. Ridge suspected she was worried the camera case would float out the truck window and travel miles downriver. Photos of a crime scene could not be retaken, especially once the body had been moved to the morgue. While the photos were important, Evan was probably concerned about the safety of the divers. Diving was treacherous. He would want to give them the best possible conditions to be successful without putting their own lives in danger.

Ridge wished he could help her understand the importance of waiting, but it would serve no purpose. She wasn't ready to listen. Not that he blamed her. A deranged person—presumably her Aunt Nikki's murderer—had attempted to take her life four times in the past forty-eight hours. In her situation, he'd want action immediately, too.

Snap out of it, Snyder! Every time you men-

tally put yourself in Jane's shoes or you feel the tug to shelter her in your arms, you weaken your ability to make the tough decisions that could mean the difference of life or death.

Ninety minutes later, Jane's freshly washed hair was wrapped in a towel, and she had put on a pair of lightweight sweatpants and an over-sized blue long-sleeved T-shirt with the word Navy printed across it in gold block letters. Justin had given the shirt to her the day he'd informed her he'd enlisted. She hadn't worn it since his death, but tonight she wanted to feel closer to him. Partly because she'd had so many near-death experiences herself recently. But mostly because she missed him, and for the first time in four years, she could think about him without crying.

Footsteps sounded on the stairway landing outside the apartment door. *Knock. Knock.* "Jane. It's Ridge."

Jane hurried across the open living space. He'd said he'd check on her later, but she'd thought he meant that he would call. She hadn't expected him to show up. Twisting the latch, she unlocked the door and opened it.

Ridge filled the doorway, wearing a pair of faded jeans and a black T-shirt, a clean-shaven face and his hair still damp from the shower. Her heart skipped a beat.

"What is it? Did something happen?"

"No. I told you I was going to check on you after you had time to clean up and change." A smile split his face. His blue eyes twinkled as he lifted the thermos he'd used to deliver coffee the day before. "I brought hot chocolate."

"The store-bought powder kind where you add hot water?" she asked, skeptical.

"No. The homemade kind our moms always made us on snowy days. With full-fat whole milk, sugar and melting chocolate."

She smiled, stepped back and opened the door wide. "Well, then, come on in."

He brushed past her, and the scent of his woodsy cologne wafted in the air. She released a slow silent breath. *Get a grip, girl. You're not in high school, and he is not your crush. You're barely friends.* Hopefully, that would change in the future. She didn't expect them to get back to the level of friendship they'd once shared— too much had happened—but it would be nice to be cordial and share details of each other's lives, even if only in passing.

"Do you want whipped cream?"

Jane glanced up and saw Ridge pull a can of whipped cream out of his back pocket. "Definitely." Giggling, she crossed to the kitchen and pulled two mugs out of the cabinet. "If I'm splurging on calories this late at night, I might as well go all in."

They settled into chairs at the table. Ridge filled each mug with the steaming chocolate liquid and topped them with a generous dome of cream. Jane lifted her mug and took a sip. The drink was like a warm hug engulfing her body. It was even better than what she remembered from childhood.

"Mmm… Don't tell my mom, but this is better than hers." Jane sat her cup down, her hands still wrapped around it as she absorbed the warmth radiating from the mug. "I need your recipe."

"Can't share it. Family secret." His smile broadened. He reached across the table and wiped the corner of her mouth with his thumb.

Jane jumped back, jolted by a wave of energy that ran through her as if she'd touched a ten-thousand-volt electric fence.

Ridge chuckled. "You had…whipped cream…"

Her face warmed, and she scrubbed the back of her hand across her mouth. "Did I get it?"

"Yeah." He nodded. Then he froze, his gaze fixated on her shirt.

Self-consciously, she glanced down. Had he just noticed it? "I…um… Justin gave it to me…"

"I remember," he whispered. "He and I went

together to buy the shirts. We each got a gray shirt for our mom that said proud Navy mom on it. And we got you and Wyatt the simple blue ones. I'm surprised you still have yours."

"I haven't worn it in years. But tonight, I wanted to feel close to him. I miss him."

"I… I'm sorry." His voice cracked, and he pushed to his feet, his face a deep crimson, tears brimming in his eyes. "I shouldn't have barged in here tonight. I'll…uh get going. You keep the chocolate."

He headed for the door. Filled with a sudden desire to hug Ridge and tell him it was okay, Jane jumped out of her seat and raced after him. Before she even realized what she was doing, her arms were around his waist in a tight embrace, her cheek pressed against his back.

"Whoa…what…" Ridge twisted, so they were facing each other.

She buried her face into his chest, inhaling the scent of his soap mingled with the woodsy sent of his cologne.

"Hey." He gently loosened her grip and stepped back, half a step, her arms still resting on his waist. "What's this all about?" he asked softly.

Unable to form words, Jane shook her head and looked at the floor, silent tears sliding down her cheeks. The look on his face when he'd noticed her shirt had ripped at her heart. She hadn't intended the shirt to be a dig at him, yet she was sure that was how he'd taken it. How did one apologize for being shortsighted and stubborn? She'd been so wrong about everything. No one was responsible for Justin joining the military but Justin himself. As for what happened on that battlefield, she was sure Ridge had done everything possible to save Justin. His actions in the river tonight proved he wouldn't leave any man—or woman—to perish. Would he ever forgive her for being so unfair to him?

Strong arms swept her off her feet and carried her across the room. He deposited her on the sofa and then settled onto the spot beside her. "Want to tell me what brought this on?" he asked after several long minutes.

Using the sleeve of her shirt, Jane dried her face. Then she sniffled and met his gaze. "I'm sorry I upset you by wearing this shirt."

"Oh, sweetie. You wearing that shirt to feel closer to Justin makes me happy."

"But you looked sad. Then you abruptly announced you were leaving." She searched his face. "I'm confused."

He sighed and scrubbed his hand over his face. Then he picked up her hand and rubbed his thumb over the back of it. "When Justin and I bought those shirts, as a way of telling our families we'd enlisted, we knew our moms would be sad to see us go. But neither one of us anticipated your reaction. You told Justin he was making the biggest mistake of his life. Then you turned on me, yelling. Telling me if I cared at all about you or your brother, I'd talk him out of following me into a career that would only lead to his death."

Her breath caught. What a horrible thing to say to someone who, next to Justin, had been her closest friend. "I forgot about that."

She closed her eyes. *Lord, give me the words to make this right.*

"I'm sorry." Opening her eyes, she continued, "Not that it's an excuse, but remember, I was young. And scared. Justin and I had never really spent much time away from each other, yet here I was headed to Colorado State and he was going to boot camp twelve hundred miles away."

"Yes. But you were right. I shouldn't have talked him into joining the Navy with me. If I hadn't, he—"

"Could have still died. In a car accident or some other way. We have no way of knowing." She met his blue eyes, determined to keep eye contact until she finished her say. "It was wrong of me to make you feel guilty that Justin joined the Navy. He was just as much of a grown man as you were. The choice was his, and his alone. And it—"

"Don't," Ridge commanded. "Don't say it."

"What?"

"Don't tell me it's not my fault that Justin died. I was the officer in charge. It was my responsibility to get my men out alive. I failed."

The pain etched on his face would have brought Jane to her knees if she hadn't already been sitting. *Dear Lord, I did that to him. I made him feel responsible. His pain is my fault. Please, let us solve this case quickly so I can go back to not seeing Ridge. Not because I don't want to have him in my life as a friend, but because I don't want to bring him any more pain.*

TEN

Ridge drew back the axe and swung with all his might. The blade hit the twelve-inch log, and the wood split right down the middle, each half falling to the ground. He leaned over, picked up one half, settled it on the old tree stump he was using as a base and split it in two. Then he repeated the process with the other half. His muscles ached, and sweat rolled down his face, stinging his eyes. Using the back of his gloved hand, he wiped the sweat off his forehead. He settled the axe against the stump, crossed to the water spigot, turned it on and picked up the hose, gulping the water as if his life depended on it. Pulling back, he lifted the hose higher and ducked his head under the stream, desperate to cool off in the extreme heat. Turning off the spigot, he looked around.

He'd split all the logs from the oak tree that had blown down near the shed in his backyard after the last snowstorm, four months ago.

The results appeared to be about half a cord—roughly four hundred pieces—of firewood for the winter. Normally, he wouldn't have engaged in an outdoor activity that could have waited until cooler weather on such a hot day. But today wasn't a normal July day. Today was the day after Jane had told him she no longer held him accountable for Justin's death.

For the past four years, he'd prayed she would forgive him. Why then did he feel even more of an ache in his heart now than he had before? *Because she didn't forgive you. She said she no longer blames you, so there was nothing to forgive. Wasn't that better than forgiveness?* Only if he'd forgiven himself.

He froze. Could he finally forgive himself? Was Jane right? Justin's decision to join the military, even if it had been at Ridge's urging, was his own? Ridge would need to spend time in prayer to work through his thoughts on the subject. For now, he needed to keep his focus on Jane.

The sun was high in the sky. It had to be nearing noon. Time had gotten away from him. He needed to check on Jane. Thankfully, she'd agreed to postpone the conference with her student until the fall semester began. Of course, it had taken very little convincing. She didn't want a repeat of yesterday any more than he did. The ranch was the safest place for her.

Now that her obligations to the college were completed for the semester, she could focus on Nikki's and Phoebe's crime scene photos. Had she started working on them yet? He didn't want to interrupt her if she had. But he also really needed to see her.

He looked toward the post and beam barn sitting in the distance. Trees obstructed most of it, but he could see the roof peeking above them. It comforted him, knowing Jane was nearby. Though it was two-tenths of a mile from his back door to the barn. Suddenly, he wished he hadn't insisted on putting his cabin so far from the other structures on the ranch. But when he'd returned home after being discharged, he'd wanted solitude. He'd been afraid his mom and brother would constantly lookout their windows, checking on his every move.

The sound of a vehicle penetrated the quiet. He walked around the side of the house and watched as Wyatt's ATV wound its way up his drive, kicking up a trail of dust behind it. As the vehicle drew near, Ridge noticed Molly sitting in her car seat beside her daddy, smiling and clapping her hands. Instantly, all the tension drained from Ridge's shoulders, as if someone had flipped a switch inside of him. No one could put a smile on his face and lighten his heart like his niece.

Wyatt pulled to a stop beside him. "Wow. You look…sweaty. And you haven't even left your house this morning. What have you been doing?"

"Splitting wood," Ridge replied, jogging around the vehicle and squatting down so he could see Molly. "Good morning, sweetheart. How's my girl?"

"Your girl." Molly lifted her arms for him to release her from the restraints.

He kissed her cheek. "I can't hold you. I'm too sweaty."

"Too sweaty," she parroted.

Ridge smiled, his heart swelling. After losing Ashlee, Wyatt had been hesitant to allow Molly to be put under anesthesia and had delayed her cochlear implant surgery until she was almost three years old. So Molly had experienced a delay in speech, but in recent months she'd begun to copy more words and sounds. He glanced at Wyatt. "Is that a new word for her?"

"Yep. Speech therapy is really helping. She's connecting more sounds. Before long, I'm sure we'll have difficulty getting her to be quiet." Wyatt beamed with pride and kissed the top of Molly's head. Then he straightened. "But the real question is why are you splitting firewood in the middle of summer? Surely, it could have waited a couple of months."

Ridge pushed to his feet and shrugged. "Had things on my mind. Figured hard work was a good way to process the thoughts."

"Jane?" Wyatt asked, one eyebrow raised.

What was with his brother's expression? Did he think Ridge was pining for Jane? "Partially. However, I highly doubt it's what you're thinking. Anyway, what brings you out here? I thought you said you had to stick close to the barn today. Isn't your prized mare about to foal?"

"Yes. Probably within the next couple of hours. But that's why I'm out here." Wyatt rested his arms on the steering wheel, his expression becoming very serious. "Grace Bradshaw stopped by to check on the expectant momma. While she was here, she mentioned seeing someone in the woods. Said they were walking along the fence line. She lost sight of them as she came up the drive."

Ridge's gut tightened. "Did she get a good look at them?"

"No. She said they stayed in the shadows. They wore a dark-colored hoodie." Wyatt shook his head. "Anyway, I've instructed the ranch hands to be on the lookout for anyone lurking around."

Dark-colored hoodie. The person after Jane always wore a black hoodie. Ridge spun on his heels and raced for his front porch. "Thanks for the information," he yelled over his shoulder.

"I'll be around if you need backup," Wyatt commanded.

"Daddy, go!" Molly squealed.

"Okay, princess."

Ridge heard Wyatt's ATV speeding away as he banged into his house, grabbed his own ATV's keys, and hurried to the small shed in the backyard where he kept it.

In a matter of minutes, Ridge was pulling to a stop beside Jane's MINI, which reminded him he needed to see if his mom would let him borrow his grandfather's old Ford truck, which they used as a ranch vehicle, until he had time to deal with the insurance company concerning his own truck. But he'd worry about all of that later. Entering the barn, he took the stairs to the apartment two at a time.

Jane met him on the landing, grinning. "Hi. I wondered when you were coming by."

Why was she on the landing? What if he had been the killer coming up the stairs? Ridge would have to talk to her about not taking chances. He took her gently by the shoulders, turned her around and ushered her inside. "Let's talk inside."

"Wait. What's wrong?" She twisted her upper body, trying to face him.

"Inside," he reiterated, his tone sharper than he'd intended. "Sorry. I just… Could we please talk inside?"

She nodded and went into the apartment without further complaint. Once they were safely inside, Ridge clicked the deadbolt into place. Then he turned and found her staring, open-mouthed.

"Are you going to tell me what's happened?" she asked, her voice scarily calm.

"Grace spotted someone lurking in the woods when she stopped by earlier," Ridge said matter-of-factly. He hated to scare her, but sugar-coating the truth would serve no purpose.

"Oh." She moved to the small kitchen table where her computer sat, settling herself on the chair in front of it.

"Is that all you have to say? *Oh?*" he demanded.

"What else is there to say?" she asked, her tone matching his. "I suspected something was up when Grace stopped by earlier and reminded me to keep the doors locked."

"She did?"

"Yeah. And I have." Jane locked eyes with him. "I'm sorry I upset you by meeting you on the landing. But I knew it was you coming up the stairs."

"How could you know that? Your windows don't overlook the front of the barn. You couldn't have seen me coming."

"No. But I know the sound of your footsteps." She caught her bottom lip between her teeth and shrugged, a gesture he'd seen many times when she was fighting back tears.

Shame washed over him. He'd been too harsh with her in his haste to lock her away and keep her safe. "I'm sorry. I didn't mean to snap at you. Your safety is my top priority."

"I know." A single tear slid down her cheek, and she hastily brushed it away.

He was instantly by her side, kneeling. "Why are you crying? I said *sorry*. In the future, I'll try to do better. I promise. It's just, I'm used to giving orders to soldiers."

She sniffled. "We all know I'm not soldier material. The one time I attempted to camp out in the backyard with you and Justin, when we were ten-year-olds, you guys tormented me. You both wanted to play army soldiers. When I didn't want to play, Justin called me a baby."

"I remember that. You were miserable."

"Yeah." She grinned. "But then I went inside and Mom let me stay up late watching movies and eating ice cream."

"I know." He chuckled. "Justin and I watched the movie through the window. We couldn't hear what the actors were saying, so we had to make up our own dialogue. It's one of my favorite childhood memories."

They sat in silence, a wave of sadness engulfing Ridge as he thought about all the life moments Justin had missed out on. Seeing how much Jane had grown, coming out of her shell, being a successful professor and forensic photographer. Although Ridge had never had such dreams, Justin had always talked about his desire to meet someone, fall in love, get married and become a dad.

Why, Lord, did I get to live but Justin didn't? Whatever the reason, Lord, I pray I live a life that is full of purpose. Starting with helping Jane solve Nikki's and Phoebe's murders, and stopping their killer before he kills Jane, too.

Jane resisted the urge to squirm as the silence stretched on, becoming increasingly awkward. Her gaze landed on the small white bag next to her laptop.

"Grace also dropped off our new cell phones." She scooted the bag closer to him.

Ridge reached into the bag, pulled out the box holding his new phone and opened it. "I didn't expect Evan to replace my phone, but I'm thankful to have it."

She shrugged. "You heard him last night. Evan felt it was his duty to replace your phone since you lost it protecting one of his employees."

"You being one of his employees has nothing to do with me protecting you."

Ridge had made it perfectly clear he was protecting her because of his guilt over Justin's death. Guilt which her own actions the past four years had added to. Would he ever be able to forgive himself?

"These phones have eSIM capability. I activated mine as soon as it arrived. All of my photos, contacts and content installed instantly, from my cloud backup. You're welcome to use my phone, or my computer, to contact your service provider to activate yours." She handed him her phone, scooted back her chair and stood. "I was just about to make myself a sandwich."

"Thanks." He smiled. "I'll take a sandwich, too, please."

"Of course." Jane crossed to the kitchen and opened the refrigerator.

Thirty minutes later, he had activated his phone and they'd eaten bacon, lettuce, tomato and avocado sandwiches.

"So, tell me. What have you been up to today?" Ridge asked.

"I'm glad you asked. I've cleaned up the images of Aunt Nikki's and Phoebe's bodies at Brush Hollow Reservoir." Suppressing a shudder, Jane motioned Ridge to come closer as she turned her computer screen for him to get a good view. She hadn't realized how hard it would be for her to see images of Nikki's dead body. Jane had only been seven years old when her dad's little sister died. And while Jane had always idolized her beautiful aunt, Nikki had been a teenager for most of Jane's life and off doing her own things.

Understandably, Jane's parents had shielded her from much of the television and news coverage, wanting to protect young Jane from being exposed to the horrid details of her aunt's death. For the longest time, they'd only told Jane that Nikki had died, and they hadn't given her any details. Then, five months after the murder, Jane was spending the night with Carolina when she overheard Uncle Leo—Jane's father's only other sibling—talking to someone on the phone, telling them the police had run out of leads.

"Did you see anything in the picture that you thought might be a clue?" Ridge asked, pulling her attention back to him.

"No, not in this photo, but…" She scrolled through the digital images she'd saved in a folder on her desktop. Finding the image of Phoebe's bedroom, she stopped. "This one. I can't pinpoint what bothers me about it, but I feel like there's a clue here waiting to be uncovered."

"Hmm… It just looks like a young woman's bedroom. Nothing appears to be out of place. The bed is made, there's a bookcase with books and knickknacks. Makeup on the dresser." Ridge, who'd settled into the chair beside her, leaned closer to the screen. "The only thing that strikes me as odd is that she didn't have any clothes scattered around. Not that I had a sister or anyone to use as a reference, but I'd think there might be something out of place."

"Exactly, my point." Jane moved to another photo, an image of Nikki's bedroom. "The bed was made, but look at the covers here."

She pointed to the corner of the bed where the blanket was wrinkled. "It looks like someone may have sat there. Could have been Nikki putting on a pair of shoes or something. Or it could have been her killer before the murders."

"Possibly." His brow furrowed. "Does anything else look out of place?"

"I'm not sure. The room isn't as tidy as Phoebe's, but I wouldn't call it messy. I thought I might see if Mom could look at it and tell me if anything looked out of place. She'd know what type of housekeeper Nikki was better than I would." She clicked out of the program and closed the computer.

"That sounds reasonable. Do you want me to get one of the ranch hands to pick her up and bring her to the ranch?"

Jane rubbed the back of her neck. The muscles in her neck and shoulders ached from hours of sitting slumped over a computer. "No. I'd rather not put her in danger by having her anywhere near me. Once I finish enhancing the last two photos, I'll send everything to Evan and let him arrange for Mom to see them."

Ridge pushed to his feet and stood behind her. "Here, let me."

He placed a hand on either side of her neck and kneaded her muscles, starting with light pressure and then gently adding more with each round of movement.

"Oh, that feels good." She closed her eyes and focused on her breathing. "I didn't know you were so talented."

"I don't advertise my skills," he said, a smile in his voice. "Otherwise, I'd have women lining up for miles, demanding a neck massage. And I don't have time for that."

"Well, then, thank you for deeming me worthy of your time." She tilted her head to one side and then the other. The muscles were already feeling much looser. "I didn't know how much I needed this. Maybe I'll treat myself to a spa day once thi—"

Her phone rang. It was the ringtone she'd set for the police station. She motioned for Ridge to stop. Then she picked up her phone and slid a finger across the screen to answer it. "Hello?"

"Jane, it's Maureen," Evan's administrative assistant, Maureen Rhodes replied. "Evan wanted me to let you know they recovered your camera bag."

"Oh, that's wonderful news!"

"He'll hand-deliver the bag to you within the next hour," Maureen continued. "Also, he wanted me to ask you to have Ridge call him."

"I'll tell him."

Jane locked eyes with Ridge, and her heart did a wonky little flip-flop. His face had a sun-kissed glow she hadn't noticed earlier. She'd been wrong in high school to think that he was handsome. Back then he had been cute. *Now* he was handsome. Muscular and masculine.

"Jane? Did you hear me?" Maureen said in her ear.

Uh-oh. Jane tightened her grip on the phone. She'd zoned out. What had she missed in the conversation? "I'm sorry. I missed that. What were you saying?"

"I said, when you get the camera and make sure everything is in working order, Evan wants you to forward copies of all images to my email. This way we'll have a backup. He doesn't want to risk anything happening to them, again."

"No problem."

"Good. Oh, and, Jane?"

"Yes?"

"Call your mother. She's worried about you. You don't have to tell her everything that's going on. Just let her know you're safe," Maureen said, her voice softening on the last sentence.

Sometimes Jane forgot how small Blackberry Falls really was. She'd hated it when she was younger and some well-meaning friend of her mother's had tried to offer advice about things Jane should or shouldn't do. But in this moment, Jane was thankful her mom had lifelong friends who would gently remind her thoughtless daughter there was someone who worried about her and needed to know she was alive and well. "Thanks, Maureen. I'll call her soon."

"Okay, then. I'll talk to you later."

"Bye." Pushing her chair away from the table, Jane stood and crossed to the window.

Ridge moved to stand beside her. "What was that all about?"

Her eyes on the horizon, she filled him in on the conversation as she watched a couple of horses run across the pasture. "…and that was it. Except for Maureen admonishing me for not calling my mom. Honestly, I have to be the world's worst daughter. I should have known Mom would hear about the things going on and be worried. Of course, she wouldn't call me because she wouldn't want me to know she's worried."

He grasped her gently by her shoulders and turned her to face him. "First off, you are not the world's worst daughter. Far from it. You gave up your career to move back to the hometown you couldn't wait to leave. Just to be near your mom after she lost your dad and Justin. That is the action of a selfless daughter. Second, you've been busy trying to stay alive. Your mom would rather you focus on that than worry about her."

Jane knew he was right, but that didn't assuage her guilt any. Even before the attacks started, she'd gotten out of the habit of talking to her mom, only checking in briefly every other week. The past few months, Mom had pushed her to get back to church and renew her relationship with the Lord. Jane hadn't wanted to have the constant reminder of her failures as a Christian, so not talking to Mom as often had been an easy out.

"If you don't mind, I'll just call Mom now. Set her mind at ease."

Picking up her phone, Jane headed toward the sleeping alcove, her footsteps faltering midway. There really wasn't anywhere to have a private conversation in the small apartment.

"I'll go down to the barn and check in with Wyatt. He's expecting a foal to be born any time now. Why don't you come down after you get off the phone?"

His thoughtfulness was like a gentle hug to her soul. "Thank you. I'll be down in a few minutes."

He tipped his head, walked out the door and closed it behind him. She crossed to the sofa and settled onto it with her feet tucked underneath her. Then she sent up a silent prayer. *Thank You, Lord, for Ridge, for his generosity and protection, and the possibility of a renewed friendship. Forgive me for turning my back on everyone in my grief and for not leaning on You to comfort me the way I should have. I will strive to do better in the future. Beginning with returning to church and no longer forsaking the assembly. You are the Hope, the Way and the*

Light. I now know I can't go through life alone, without You and friends by my side.

Pressing the phone icon on her cell, she quickly dialed her mom's number and pressed the call button.

"Hi, Jane," her mom answered on the second ring. "I'm so glad you called."

"Me, too, Mom. Sorry it's been so long…"

ELEVEN

Leaning against the door to the stall, Ridge held Molly where she could see the colt that had been born just before he arrived downstairs twenty minutes ago.

"Baby. Sweet baby," Molly chanted, stretching out her arm toward the wobbly legged foal.

"He is sweet. But not as sweet as you are." Ridge kissed his niece's neck, pretending like he was going to gobble her up.

She responded with giggles, pulling away from him and then leaning in, begging, "More."

"Am I interrupting?" Jane asked from behind them.

Ridge lifted his head and smiled. "No. We're just playing a game and admiring the newest baby on the ranch."

"Oh, it's here." Jane pressed in beside them and peered into the small area where the new mom and baby were resting. "Oh, he's beautiful."

Molly reached out, slid her hand up Jane's

arm and touched her shoulder. Jane turned and Molly dove into her arms. "Pretty."

Jane balanced Molly on her hip and turned to show her the colt. "Yes, he is pretty."

"No." Molly touched Jane's face. "You're pretty."

Ridge watched as surprise registered on Jane's face. She smiled. "And you are a beautiful princess."

Molly giggled.

"It's past the princess's nap time," Wyatt said, walking up to them. He gave Jane a quick side-hug. "Hi, Jane. I hope you are comfortable in the apartment."

"I am. Thank you."

"Let us know if you need anything. And don't worry about the person Grace saw lurking near the entrance earlier. We've ordered the ranch hands to stay armed and alert."

"Thank you." She scrunched her nose. "I'm sorry that I've brought danger to the ranch."

"If there's any danger, we'll handle it. The main thing is to keep you safe," Ridge interjected.

"Agreed." Wyatt held his hands out to his daughter. "Okay, princess. Nap time."

"No." Molly pressed her cheek against Jane's and held on tightly. "Stay."

Jane hugged Molly. "I'm so glad I got to see

you, Molly. Maybe we can have a tea party some time, if it's okay with your dad."

"Tea party!" Molly demanded.

"Oh, you've done it now." Wyatt smiled. "She loves tea parties."

"Don't most little girls?" Jane pried Molly's arms loose and handed her to her father. Then she kissed Molly's cheek. "I'll come see you soon."

"Okay, princess. Let's get you home." Wyatt rubbed Molly's back and made his way down the center aisle of the barn. Molly laid her head on her dad's shoulder and waved goodbye, her eyelids heavy.

"She is so precious." Jane turned to Ridge, her eyes shining.

Ridge caught his breath. He would never marry or have children of his own. He'd made that decision long ago, during one of his parents' last fights. Marriage was hard, and the kids were the ones caught in the middle when the parents didn't know how to communicate.

His dad's untimely death had solidified his decision. Years later, meeting children left behind by soldiers killed in combat reinforced it. Whether the parent died in an anger-induced car accident or defending the country, growing up without a parent was just as difficult as growing up with parents who fought over issues like money or staying out late.

If Ridge were the marrying kind, he'd want a wife who looked at their children the same way Jane had looked at Molly. *No. Don't let your mind go there. Your life is perfect the way it is. You can play with Molly and spoil her, then send her back home without having to worry that you might mess up her life.*

"How'd the call go with your mom?" he asked, changing the subject.

"It was good. And even though I don't think Aunt Nikki's killer would have a reason to go after Mom, I told her to be extra diligent about locking her doors and to call the police if she saw anyone hanging around nearby."

"I hope she heeds your words."

"She will." Jane's brow furrowed, and a frown marred her face.

"What's wrong?"

"I'm wondering… I think…" She puffed out a breath. "I think I need to move off the ranch."

"What? No. You can't do—"

"Please, hear me out," she said softly, dousing his anger.

He pressed his lips together and nodded. "Okay."

"When I first accepted your offer of a place to stay, I only planned to be here for one night.

But it's been three. And now it seems like Nikki's and Phoebe's killer has tracked me here. If anything were to happen to Molly, or your mom, or—"

"Nothing is going to happen to them. *Or you.* As long as you're on this ranch, I will protect you and everyone else on the property." The thought of her going somewhere else, out of his sight, sent chills down his spine. He could not allow that to happen. Whatever it took, he had to convince her she was safer here than anywhere else. And if he couldn't, then he'd have to convince her to let him go with her wherever she went.

A door slammed and footsteps sounded from the short hall at the foot of the stairs leading to the apartment. Ridge stepped in front of Jane, his hand instantly going for the gun in his waistband.

Evan stepped into the open. "Sorry, folks. Didn't mean to startle you, but thought it might be best to make my presence known. Seemed like you two were in a heated discussion."

Ridge holstered his weapon. Heated discussions were the conversations his parents had always engaged in. This was not like that. It was a man desperately trying to talk sense into his oldest friend. "Just trying to convince Jane she's safest if she stays put."

"Yes. I heard." Evan stopped beside Jane, handing over her still-soggy camera bag. "There was about a half inch of water inside. I dumped it out, but left everything inside the way you had it. Hopefully, the moisture didn't reach the SD card."

"Thanks. I'll check it out when I get upstairs." She accepted the bag and looked down at the floor.

Ridge felt like a heel. Jane had never liked confrontations, but even more, she hated for other people to know her business.

Evan cleared his throat. "Why don't we go upstairs and discuss our options? If Jane feels unsafe here, maybe we should move her."

Ridge clenched his fist at his side. He did not want to discuss moving Jane elsewhere, but when it came right down to it, he didn't have any right to say so. Jane glanced at him, then motioned for Evan to follow her. They walked to the stairs and began the assent upward. Evan looked in Ridge's direction and jerked his head, sending a silent message for him to follow.

Lord, grant me the wisdom to know when to speak up and when to remain silent. When I do voice my concerns, please let me do so in a manner that encourages Jane to listen and not shut down. Amen.

* * *

Jane felt heat creeping up her neck as she climbed the stairs. Her face, neck and ears would be a deep shade of red by now. Sometimes, she wished she could have been more like Justin. He'd been the twin who spoke up when he didn't like something. The one people listened to. She knew both Ridge and Evan were concerned for her safety. So was she. But she could not allow concern for her own safety to put others at risk, especially Molly.

Entering the apartment, she crossed to the kitchen table and sat the camera bag down. *Please, Lord, let the SD card be undamaged. As much as I'd hate having to replace it, the camera is replaceable. The photos I took last night are not.*

Jane unzipped the bag. It appeared the water had seeped into the bag around the zipper. The inside of the bag was damp to the touch, but the camera appeared mostly dry. Evan had said there had been a half inch of water in the bag. She held her breath and lifted the camera. Her heart sank. The display screen, which had been sitting against the bottom of the bag, was wet, as were the sides of the camera, including the SD slot and all the various ports. Depressing the release button, she pulled the SD card out. It was damp, but that didn't mean all was lost.

"I've got to get this dry." She glanced at the two men flanking her, no longer concerned about the argument Evan had overheard or the discussion still to be had about her safety.

"What do you need? Rice?" Evan asked.

"No." Jane shook her head. "That only dries the surface level. And small particles and dust from the rice can actually cause more damage."

She turned to look at Ridge. "Do you have any rubbing alcohol?"

"I'm sure there's some in the tack room." He headed for the door. "I'll go grab some."

"Thanks," she yelled after him.

"Do you think you can save it?" Evan asked.

"I'm sure going to try." She placed the SD card on the table, picked up the camera and crossed to the kitchen, opened a drawer and withdrew a cotton tea towel. Then she dried the exterior of the camera.

"Do you want to tell me what prompted your desire to move off the ranch?" Evan asked.

"I saw Molly today." Her voice cracked. She paused, taking a deep breath.

Standing patiently, Evan waited for her to continue. She met his gaze.

"If anything happened to her because of me… I can't stay here."

"I understand," he replied. "I'll see what I

can arrange. Can you stay here until I figure out where to relocate you?"

"I was hoping you'd ask the Vincents if they would allow me to stay at the cabin on their ranch, where you and Grace stayed when her life was in danger."

"That might be an option, only—"

"What might be an option?" Ridge asked, walking into the apartment.

Jane had been so focused on her discussion with Evan she'd failed to hear Ridge coming back up the stairs. Emboldened by the knowledge Evan didn't think her desire to move was an overreaction, she squared her shoulders and faced Ridge. "Moving to the cabin on the Vincents' property."

He nodded, handed her the gallon-size jug he carried. "Sorry. We don't have any smaller sizes."

"This is fine. Thanks." She took the offering, shocked that he'd accepted her decision to move without further argument.

She poured some of the rubbing alcohol onto the tea towel and wiped down the SD card. Placing the SD card on the counter, she wiped down the camera, removed the battery, and opened all covers to provide as much air circulation inside as possible. "There's a small portable fan on a shelf in the bedroom alcove. Could one of you grab it for me?"

"I'll get it," Ridge volunteered.

Jane met Evan's gaze, and her boss shrugged. Apparently, she wasn't the only one confused by Ridge's lack of reaction. He returned with the fan in hand, plugged it into an outlet and placed it on the table.

Jane placed the camera and SD card in front of the circulating air and stepped back. "Well, that's all I can do for now. I'll give the SD card a couple of hours to dry, then I'll test it out."

"Don't forget to send copies to Maureen," Evan reminded her.

"I won't. If I can retrieve the photos, that is."

"Okay, I'll get going." Evan made eye contact with her. "I'll let you know as soon as I get the details worked out about the other location."

"We'll be ready," Ridge replied before Jane could.

She furrowed her brow. "What does that mean?"

"Exactly what I said. *We'll be ready.*"

Jane lifted her hands, palms outward, and shrugged. She needed more information.

Ridge exhaled. "You didn't think you were going without me, did you? What if the person who's trying to kill you finds you there? Blackberry Falls isn't really large enough for you to hide anywhere without being found. And you know it."

"But what about the ranch? You're needed here. Your mom and Wyatt depend on you to do your share around here."

"They can make do without me for a few days—"

"And this is where I came in," Evan announced, reminding them of his presence.

The familiar heat crept up her neck again, and she pressed her lips together.

"I will show myself out so you two can continue this discussion." He placed a hand on her shoulder. "For what it's worth, Ridge is right. Wherever you hide, you need someone—preferably with a gun—to stay with you and protect you."

Evan patted her shoulder, shook hands with Ridge and walked out without another word. She bit her lip. It didn't look like she would win this argument. And in all honesty, she hadn't been looking forward to being alone in a cabin in the woods. Normally, she wasn't a person easily frightened. Her recent near-death experiences had been unnerving, but being alone in a cabin with Ridge was equally unnerving. Not simply because their renewed friendship was still fragile. It had more to do with her reaction at seeing him when he'd arrived at the barn today. As she'd worked on the Brush Hollow Reservoir photos that morning, she'd jumped with excitement every time she heard a noise in the barn, thinking it was *him* coming to see her.

The wall she'd built around her heart when he'd rejected her after high school graduation, and that she'd cemented even more firmly into place after Justin's funeral, had suffered several fractures in its foundation the past few days. Even though she no longer held resentment toward him over Justin's death, and a small door of friendship had opened, she didn't want the entire wall to collapse. Because if it did, she didn't know if she'd be able to stop her childhood crush from reigniting, and that would serve no purpose for anyone, least of all her.

"Do you have to stand so closely?" Jane asked Ridge, for what seemed like the hundredth time, several hours later as she sorted through the photos from the SD card, which thankfully had been unharmed by the small amount of moisture that had reached it. "I promise, I'll show you the photos as soon as I have them all uploaded."

Ridge sank into the chair opposite her at the small dining table. "I'm just bored. Isn't there anything I can do to help?"

A smile crept on her face, and she quickly

captured her lips between her teeth to stop it from spreading. He wouldn't be happy if she laughed at him, but he sounded so much like ten-year-old Ridge at the moment. A natural-born fidgeter, he'd always gotten bored easily. Which had led to some trouble for both him and Justin, especially the time they'd built a tree house without asking permission.

The boys had built it in the oak tree in Jane and Justin's backyard. By her brother's logic, it had only made sense that the tree house be in their yard since Jane would want to hang out in it, too. And two against one meant Justin—and Jane—would have primary ownership of the tree house. They'd helped themselves to some of the lumber her dad had planned to use to build raised flower beds for her mom. Needless to say, none of the parents were happy with their decision.

She caught sight of Ridge in her peripheral vision. He'd moved to the kitchen area and was opening and closing cabinets. What was he searching for?

"Why don't you make us some coffee?" she asked.

"Isn't it kind of late in the day for coffee? I'll be up all night if I have a lot of caffeine this time of day."

Jane giggled, no longer able to contain her

laughter. "You sound like an old man. You know there's such a thing as decaffeinated coffee, right? Your mom sent over a few pantry staples the day after I arrived. She included both caffeinated and decaffeinated coffee. It's in the cabinet to your left."

He looked at her and frowned. "But it's ninety degrees outside. Do you really want hot coffee?"

"Sure, I do. I'm like my dad. I can drink hot coffee twenty-four seven, three-hundred-sixty-five days a year. It won't faze me, or keep me awake." She smiled.

"Fine. I'll make you a cup. I'm sure my mom also included coffee pods in her delivery. No need making a full pot if I'm not drinking any." He opened the cabinet. "Any preference on flavor?"

"Nope."

She turned back to the computer and focused on her task while he was busy with his own. In the short time it took him to make her coffee, she finished the upload, attached all the images to an email and sent them to Evan and Maureen.

Ridge placed a steaming cup of coffee in front of her. "Cream. No sugar."

"Just the way I like it." She picked up the mug and took a sip. "This is good. Thank you."

"You're welcome." He sat in the chair beside her, a cold soda in his hand. "I found this in the fridge."

"Yeah, the sodas were there when I arrived."

"We have a smaller college-dorm size fridge in the tack room, but we keep extra snacks and drinks up here, too. On days when there are riding classes going on or, like today, when there's a mare in labor or something, it's easier to run upstairs for a sandwich or snack than it is to go back to our individual homes."

The day before, Jane had stood at the picture window that allowed light into the main living area and watched as Wyatt had given riding lessons to children who appeared to be between the ages of five and ten. The laughter from the children, along with the encouragement she'd witnessed from Wyatt and the parents present, had eased the stress she'd felt and temporarily allowed her to forget her own troubles. "Wyatt's riding lessons are for kids with special needs?"

"Yes. Using his degree in psychology and his knowledge of horses, he's developed an equine therapy program specifically for children who struggle with social cues or forming strong relationships. He's also working on a new program designed to help children who have suffered trauma—physical or emotional."

"You sound very proud of him."

"Oh, I am."

"I'm sorry my being here has disrupted his routine."

"Wyatt having to go home for a sandwich at lunchtime is not a major disruption." He laced his fingers around his drink. "I understand your desire to move to the Vincents' cabin. You're worried about Molly, which I appreciate. I actually agree with the move, if Evan can work out the details, since your location here appears compromised."

"But?" Why was he taking so long to get to his point?

"I can't force you to continue to accept my protection, but will you, *please*, allow me to accompany you to the cabin?" Ridge looked at her expectantly.

"Thank you for asking, and not demanding that I do what you want." She moistened her lips. "I agree with you and Evan. I need someone with me that has a gun and knows how to use it. Not that I want anyone to lose their life, but I also don't want to die at the hands of a murderer."

He released a breath, his shoulders visibly relaxing. "If I'm not mistaken, the Vincents are on their annual trip to Tennessee to visit their daughter, Bridget, and her family. I'm sure Evan has their number, though, so maybe he can still get everything worked out so we can move tomorrow."

She hoped he was right. The sooner she could steer the danger away from Rustic Roots Ranch and Ridge's family, the better.

TWELVE

"**W**ow. It's amazing that you can use editing software to sharpen blurry images like that." Ridge leaned back from the computer screen. "There's no issue using the enhanced photos in court?"

Jane looked at him aghast. "Why would there be?"

"Well, I'm not saying you would do this to the photos, but couldn't the defense argue that the photos were manipulated and therefore they could be tainted?"

"They could. That's why the prosecution always calls experts to validate the process."

"Makes sense. Did you notice anything in the photographs that the police might have missed during the original investigation?"

"Not really. Of course, Evan will have a better idea of important details once he's gone over all of Gordon Davidson's notes. And it's quite possible the notebook they found in his possession may have additional information not included in the original investigation notes. Seems like the unsolved murders troubled him."

She clicked to the photographs of Phoebe's bedroom. Zooming in on an image of the bookcase, she pointed to the lone bookend. "This strikes me as odd."

"A queen chess piece statue?" Ridge turned to her. "What's odd about that? Phoebe obviously liked to play chess."

"Look at it closer. It's a bookend."

"Okay, so?"

"So, where is the other one? I did an online search. They sold these in pairs. A king and a queen. Where's the king?"

"It looks like it's carved from stone. I imagine it would be very heavy. Could it have been the murder weapon?"

"No. Both women were strangled. Investigators recovered the murder weapon with the bodies. It was a nylon strap, still wrapped around Phoebe's neck. Fibers from the strap were also present on Nikki's neck."

Ridge was impressed she knew so many details. "You've really studied this case, haven't you?"

"Yes." She clicked out of the software program, powered off and closed the laptop. "Grandma Mason's advancing dementia diagnosis two years ago inspired me to look into the case. I hope to give her the answers she's always searched for. Before she no longer remembers anything about Aunt Nikki. Although, forgetting her youngest child and her murder might be a blessing."

Ridge placed a hand over hers and squeezed. He remembered the feeling of helplessness when his Grandfather Ramsey's health was declining. Nothing had prepared him for losing the patriarch of his mother's family. "I know it's hard to see your grandmother's health decline. How is she doing at the moment? Does she remember you and your mom?"

"On her *good days*, she will, but most days, no." She patted his hand covering hers. "Thanks for asking."

"I heard she'd moved in with your mom after your dad passed. Is your mom her sole caregiver?"

Jane tugged her hand free from his grasp. "No. Unfortunately, Grandma Mason developed a tendency to wander off. As much as Mom hated the idea of not being the one to take care of Dad's mother, she had to make the difficult decision to move her to an assisted living facility that specializes in Alzheimer's and dementia care."

Jane stood and carried her mug to the sink.

Then she picked up the cardboard pizza box with half the pepperoni and sausage pizza that he'd had delivered hours earlier still inside, and she put it into the fridge. "Guess breakfast will be leftovers."

"Sounds like a feast to me." He glanced out the window. The night sky had turned a deep ebony color, clouds blocking the stars and moon. "If you've been searching for answers for two years, have you compiled a list of suspects?"

"No. I've questioned all the faculty and staff on campus that worked there when Nikki and Phoebe were students. According to Evan, they all had alibis for the night the girls were murdered. And none of my conversations with them turned up anything new. If only I would have asked to see the crime scene photos two years ago. The case might have been solved by now." She leaned against the counter and folded her arms across her waist. "I guess I'm not much of a sleuth. Good thing I make my living with photography and not investigation."

"You're not expected to solve a twenty-three-year-old crime all by yourself."

With a sigh, he stood and tossed his soda bottle into the recycling bin. "It's late. I'd better get out of here so you can get some rest. Tomorrow is likely to be a long day. If we move you to the

Vincents' property, we'll have to take the long route and ensure no one follows us. We'll also have to coordinate with Evan to have supplies brought to the cabin, possibly using decoys to throw anyone watching off the trail."

"You sound like you're planning a military mission."

"Only far more important, since your life is the one at stake here." He met her eyes. "I will take whatever steps necessary to be successful."

Impulsively, he bent and kissed the top of her head, the scent of honeysuckles filling his nose. As he straightened, she wrapped her arms around his waist and hugged him tightly.

"Thank you for being by my side," she whispered. "I know you're doing it out of a sense of obligation—a fill-in for Justin. But I would be dead by now, multiple times over, if not for you and your quick thinking."

Ridge returned the embrace. He may have originally felt an obligation to Justin. That was no longer the case. Even if Justin were around, Ridge would still fight to stay by Jane's side until he knew, without a doubt, she was safe. Which he hoped would be soon.

The way his heart drummed in his chest when she hugged him close, he wasn't sure he'd be able to keep his heart from further involvement if they had to spend too many more days together. The sooner they captured the killer, the better off Ridge's heart would be. He'd be able to put some distance between him and Jane, allowing him the ability to remind himself they were simply childhood friends, nothing more.

He reached behind his back, grasped her hands and loosened her grip on him. Then he stepped out of her embrace. "I'm sleeping in the tack room tonight. Yell, if you need me."

"What? I'm sure there's no need for that."

"Like you said, I'm a former SEAL on a mission. Can't risk the person lurking at the edge of the property getting past the boundary and reaching you."

"But the tack room can't be comfortable. Go to your cabin. *Like you said*, tomorrow will be a long day. You need a good night's rest, too. I'll call you if I hear anything suspicious."

He pursed his lips and slowly shook his head. "Not happening. Besides, I had Wyatt put a cot in the tack room for me. It'll be fine. I've slept in worse conditions."

"I still thi—"

"Good night, Jane." He crossed to the door, opened it and glanced over his shoulder. "Lock the door behind me."

Ridge stepped out onto the landing and pulled the door closed behind him, waiting until he heard the deadbolt click into place before he proceeded down the stairs. When he reached the ground floor, he went to the stall where the new mama and baby rested. The mare stood admiring her foal as he rested at her feet. When she noticed Ridge standing at the door, she ambled over to him and nudged him with her muzzle.

He rubbed the soft fur along her nose. "You did a good job bringing that handsome boy into the world."

Neigh. The mare nodded her head as if in agreement with him.

"You have a right to be proud." He ran his hand through the mare's mane. "Hang on. I bet Wyatt has treats in the tack room."

He crossed the wide hall to the tack room that sat diagonally to the mare's stall. Attracted by the sounds of movement, the other horses—seven in total—each stuck their heads out of their individual stalls. Ridge laughed. "Okay, late-night treats for everyone."

Soon, he'd given the new mama an apple and each of the other horses a carrot. Then he turned off the overhead lights. Night lights along the edge of the concrete floor offered enough lighting to guide his steps to the tack room. Leaving the door open, he located a small oscillating fan and settled it on the countertop. Then he angled the fan to direct the air toward the cot. Removing his holstered gun, he lay it on a shelf, within reach, and then he stretched out on the cot, fully dressed, boots and all. Puffing out a breath, he placed his hands behind his head with his fingers laced together and stared up at the ceiling.

Lord, I've had tough missions in remote locations. Some were a success, and some were failures. Sometimes we all came home. Sometimes we didn't—good men losing their lives, giving all they had for their country.

An image of Justin smiling as he completed an obstacle course during basic training flashed in his mind's eye. After their completion of the BUD/S (Basic Underwater Demolition/SEAL) training, Justin had told Ridge he'd never worked so hard or been prouder of his own accomplishments in his entire life. Ridge wished Jane could have seen her brother in that setting. Ridge may have encouraged Justin to join the military with him, but Justin's success as a SEAL was all his own. He'd had a goal and the motivation necessary to complete it. In the end, it had cost him his life. But Ridge knew deep down that, even if Justin had known the outcome, he would have still joined the military and fought for his country.

If he'd known there would come a day his

sister needed protection from a killer, would he have still joined? Probably not. There was no one on this earth Justin loved more than his twin. *Lord, I pray I can fill his shoes and protect her the way he would have. In Christ's most holy name, amen.*

Bang! Bang! Bang! "Come on, Jane, wake up!"

Jane bolted upright in bed, her heart hammering in her chest. "Ridge? What's wrong?"

"Fire! The barn is on fire!"

She jumped out of bed and raced, barefooted, across the smooth wood floor, past the small kitchen and dining area and through the living room. What had he said? The barn is on fire? Fumbling with the lock, it took her a second to get her fingers to do as her brain ordered. Finally, she unlocked the door and threw it open.

Ridge brushed past her, smoke billowing in behind him. "All the barn doors have been barricaded. I can't get them open. We've got to find another way out."

"What about Wyatt? Can he try to reach us from the outside?" she asked, struggling to keep the panic out of her voice.

"I called him. And nine-one-one. Wyatt can't leave Molly alone. He's taking her to Mom's house. I estimate it will take him about five minutes, minimum, to get here. And it will take the fire department at least fifteen minutes to reach us. Each minute counts. We're on our own. And we have animals depending on us, too."

His words were like a cold bucket of ice water being dumped over her head, shocking but also sending her into high alert. "What do we do?"

"Best I can tell, the fire circles the entire barn. The only way out will be from one of these upstairs windows." Ridge raced from window to window. Reaching the sleeping alcove, he climbed onto the bed and peered out the window that was partially covered by the headboard. "We'll go out this way. A big limb of the oak tree stretches over the rooftop. We can shimmy along it and then climb down."

"You do it. I'll meet you downstairs and go out the door after you get it open." She could not do what he asked. It had been twenty years since she'd shimmied up or down a tree.

He jumped off the bed and pushed it to the side. "We go…*hrrumph*…together."

"But I ca—"

He spun and grasped her firmly by the shoulders. "You can. And you will. I'm not leaving here without you."

The sounds of horses neighing and kicking

their stall walls drifted from below. He tightened his grip and locked eyes with hers. "Do it for the horses…the new colt… He's depending on you."

She moistened her lips, her throat parched. "Okay."

He glanced down at her feet. "Put shoes on. The roof is metal and will be hot from the heat of the fire."

Jane hurriedly located her sneakers, shoved her feet into them and tied the laces. If she stopped to think about what she was about to do, she wasn't sure she could go through with it. When they were younger, she had always acted tough in front of Justin and Ridge, because she never wanted them to think less of her. She wasn't so sure she could pull that off tonight.

"Ready?" Ridge asked, pulling her from her thoughts. He unlocked the window and pushed it and the screen upward, then he turned to her, his hand outstretched.

"As I'll ever be." She placed her hand in his and let him guide her to the window.

He pointed to a limb about eight inches in diameter that stretched over the edge of the roof. "Once you get to the limb, I want you to make your way across it—sitting or lying on your stomach and scooting, whatever works for you. Position yourself as close to the tree trunk as you can, so when I get on the branch all the weight isn't on one end."

The metal gulf between her and the tree limb might as well have been the width of the Atlantic Ocean. Her throat tightened, and tears stung her eyes. She shook her head. "No. I can't. I'll fall."

"No, you won't," Ridge assured her. "We spent our childhood training for this moment."

"But…" Her body shook uncontrollably.

Ridge pulled her into a tight embrace. "Whoa. It's okay. I'm right here with you."

The tears poured freely now, her anxiety taking over.

"Okay, new plan." Ridge pulled back and brushed away her tears. "I'll go out the window first. You follow right behind me, holding onto me as I walk us both to the tree branch. Then we get off the roof together."

Wood splintering and high-pitched neighs from below penetrated her brain. *Move, Jane. Save the horses.*

"Okay. Go!" she urged.

Ridge pushed through the open window, stood and turned, holding out both his hands. "Give me your hands. Try not to touch the roof, except with your shoes. It's too hot and will burn your flesh."

She stuck her upper body through the opening and placed her hands in his. He gripped her hands tightly and pulled her through the window opening in an upright position, settling her firmly on the roof. Heat penetrated the soles of her shoes, and she feared the rubber was melting.

Smoke filled the air. She coughed and waved her hand in front of her face, desperate to clear her vision.

"Get on my back," Ridge demanded.

"What? That wasn't the plan."

"Now!" Without waiting for a reply, he turned away from her, executing a maneuver she'd never seen before, and hoisted her onto his back. "Hold on and don't let go."

She gasped and hooked her arms around his neck and her legs around his waist, holding on tightly as he ran across the roof at a slight angle. Ridge dove for the tree. Jane closed her eyes, releasing a piercing scream as he went airborne. They stopped with a jolt. She opened her eyes. Ridge had grasped the limb midway between the roof and the trunk of the tree. They were dangling in the air.

Jane looked down and quickly glanced up again. If they fell, they would likely both end up with broken bones. Or worse. "What do we do now?" she asked.

Ridge puffed out a breath. "I get us out of

this tree." He let go of the tree with one hand and swung forward, grasping the branch farther along its length. Then he repeated the process, alternating hands, until he reached the trunk where three sections merged into one, creating a V.

"You need to climb off now," he instructed, turning so she'd be closer to the trunk.

She hoisted herself into the V and then shimmied down the trunk, Ridge close behind. A king cab farm truck barreled to a stop in front of the barn, Wyatt and Mrs. Snyder climbing out of it.

"We've got to get the horses out!" Ridge yelled, running over to them. "Mom, stay with Jane in the truck. We don't know if the person who started the fire is still around."

"Okay." Mrs. Snyder wrapped an arm around Jane.

"No. We need to help get the horses out. The colt that was born today." Jane tried to pull free.

"Stay with Mom. Once we get the door open, you can help if it's not too dangerous," Ridge said, opening the back door of the truck and urging her inside.

She slid inside, scooting over so Mrs. Snyder could climb in beside her. Ridge hit the lock button on the door and slammed it closed. Jane watched as Wyatt unraveled a water hose attached to a metal pipe that stuck up out of the ground near the watering trough. He turned the water on and started spraying the large double doors at the front of the barn. Wyatt yelled something to Ridge, and he raced to the truck and started digging through the tool chest in the truck bed.

"If anything happens to the horses, it will be all my fault." Jane buried her face in her hands. She hadn't left the Snyder ranch soon enough. She hadn't thought to be worried about the animals, her concern mostly for Molly and the rest of the family. Jerking upward, she met Mrs. Snyder's eyes. "Wait. Where's Molly? What if the killer goes after her to get to me and Ridge?"

"Molly's fine, dear. She's asleep at my house. Jake and Fern are with her. They won't let anyone harm her."

Jake and Fern Potter were husband and wife and had worked for Rustic Roots Ranch for as long as Jane could remember. Jake was the ranch foreman and Fern was the housekeeper and cook. They lived in a small cottage close to the main house. Ridge had always said they were more like family than employees. Jane suspected they would do anything to protect little Molly.

"Now stop feeling sorry for yourself," Mrs.

Snyder chided. "It's horrible what's happening to you, but none of this is your fault. You don't have control over other people's actions." She smiled and patted Jane's hand. "Besides, I trust my sons to get the horses out safely. Wyatt installed a sprinkler system in the barn. I'm sure it's activated by now."

Jane shifted her attention back to the brothers. Wyatt had put out the section of fire in front of the doors and Ridge was using bolt cutters to cut the chain that had been locked into place to prevent their easy escape. Wyatt dropped the hose and he and Ridge opened the doors and disappeared inside.

Before Mrs. Snyder could stop her, Jane unlocked the door, scrambled out of the back seat and raced into the barn. As Mrs. Snyder had predicted, the sprinkler system was working and water rained down on Jane. Wyatt had a halter on a beautiful quarter horse and was escorting him out of the barn.

"Where's Ridge?" Jane searched for him through the smoke and haze.

"Taking care of the mare and foal." Wyatt brushed past her, handing off the horse to his mom who'd followed Jane into the barn.

She rushed to Ridge's side. He had put a halter on the mare, but the colt was fighting him.

Jane pushed into the stall. "Do you think he'd follow her out if we led her?"

"I do, but I'm concerned some of the other horses might hurt him in their haste to get out of the smoke." He brushed sweat from his brow with his forearm.

"What if I lead her and you carry the colt?" She coughed and fanned smoke away from her face.

"I think that's probably our best option." Ridge held out the reins. "Slow and steady. We want her to keep her baby in her sights."

Jane nodded and took the reins, holding them tightly as Ridge bent and scooped the long-legged colt into his arms. Soon he led them into the open air toward a large round pen where the horses, those already removed from the barn, neighed and ran free, bucking and kicking.

Ridge shook his head and moved to a hitching post outside the pen. Placing the colt on the ground, he took the reins from Jane and looped them around the post so the mare was secure. "They should be fine here. The colt isn't likely to leave his mama."

As if to prove his point, the colt stood and wobbled over to the mare. *Thank You, Lord, for keeping the animals safe.*

"Get back in the truck. I'm going to help remove the rest of the horses."

"No, I'll help."

The sound of sirens broke through the animal sounds and Jane turned to see Evan's patrol vehicle come up the drive, a fire truck close behind. Evan slammed to a stop in front of them, gravel spitting out from under his SUV's tires. Then he and Grace exited the vehicle and rushed over to them.

"Go get the rest of the horses out," Grace ordered. "I'll take over here."

"Thanks, Doc." Ridge glanced at Jane, frowned and raced back into the barn.

"How many more horses are in there?" Evan asked.

Jane quickly counted the horses she could see. "Maybe two."

Mrs. Snyder and Wyatt walked through the smoky opening, each escorting a horse into the fresher air. Ridge took the reins from his mom, saying something to her that caused her to look their way. She nodded and headed toward them as the firefighters worked to unwind the hose on the tanker truck.

Jane turned to Evan. "I need to leave here immediately. I will not bring more danger to this family."

She wasn't taking anything but a resounding yes from her boss. No matter what Ridge might say about it later.

THIRTEEN

Ridge stepped out of the bathroom, freshly shaven and clean. It was amazing what a hot shower could do to rejuvenate a body. Now, to go find Jane. His mom had taken her to the main house while the firefighters had worked to put out the fire. He hoped she'd been able to get a nap. Evan had told Ridge that Jane was more determined than ever to leave the ranch. He couldn't say he blamed her.

He'd always thought the ranch was one of the safest places on earth, but it seemed they needed to reevaluate and install an up-to-date security system with a lot of cameras. Some horses on the ranch were valuable and brought in a good amount of money in stud fees. They couldn't risk anyone harming or stealing them. Thankfully, they housed those animals in a different barn than the horses used for Wyatt's therapy school. Not that the horses used for therapy weren't valuable. They were. But if all the horses on the ranch had been housed in the same barn, it would have been unlikely that they would have gotten them all out without injury.

Only now they faced the task of finding temporary homes for the horses that were displaced. And Wyatt would have to suspend riding classes for the foreseeable future as they rebuilt the barn.

It had taken the firefighters a couple of hours to get the fire completely under control. Thankfully, the sprinkler system Wyatt had installed during the building process had helped save the horses, but the damage to the structure had been extensive.

Picking up his cell phone off his dresser, he navigated to his recent calls list and pressed the icon to call his mom. She answered on the second ring.

"Hi, Mom. I wanted to check and see if Jane was awake but didn't want to call her phone in case she was resting."

"No, she didn't sleep. After she got cleaned up, she's been playing with Molly and now she's cooking breakfast for everyone while I call around to our neighbors to see if they have space for any of our horses."

"Okay, well then, I'm about to head up to the house. Could you ask Jane if she needs anything?"

"My camera and laptop!" Jane yelled from the background. "If it's possible."

"I'm sure you heard that. Guess I should have told you I had you on speaker," Mom said, a smile in her voice.

"Yeah, that would have been the considerate thing to do." He laughed. "But it's okay. I won't hold it against you."

"Thanks, son." She giggled. "Why don't you head on over? By the smell of things, breakfast is almost ready."

"Five minutes," Jane declared.

"I'll see you soon." He disconnected the call.

Ridge retrieved Jane's laptop, camera bag and cell phone from his bed, where he had left them earlier. He was glad he'd asked the firefighters to grab them when they used the ladder truck to reach the second floor and check for any remaining embers. Of course, all the items had been wet, but he'd dried them off to the best of his ability. And he had no doubt that Jane would have some tricks up her sleeve to ensure that they were thoroughly dried and in working order once again. Unfortunately, he hadn't thought to ask the firefighters to gather any other items, like clothing, but that was a minor issue that could be easily rectified. He was sure his mother had some things Jane could wear. Or he could ask Grace Bradshaw to pick up some items for her.

He slung the camera bag strap over his shoulder. Then he went into the kitchen, grabbed a canvas grocery bag out of the cabinet and slid the laptop and cell phone into it. Making his way outside, he jumped into his ATV and sped down his drive. As he turned into his mom's driveway, a vehicle came from the direction of the main gate. He shaded his eyes. A green Subaru Forester. He didn't recognize the vehicle, but his mom had posted ranch hands around the property, including one at the main gate, to keep eyes on everything. It was unlikely the person approaching was anything other than a friend. Still, he'd wait for them at the end of the drive just to be sure. Pulling the ATV sideways, blocking his mother's driveway, he waited.

The vehicle drew near, and he released a sigh of relief when Jane's cousin Carolina pulled to a stop, smiling and waving from the driver's seat. Ridge exited the ATV and walked over to the vehicle as she rolled down her window.

"I thought you were on vacation. When did you get back?" he asked.

"Yesterday. Aunt Cindy called this morning and asked me to bring Jane some clothes."

"I'm sure Jane will appreciate that."

Carolina furrowed her brow. "It was unsettling to arrive home and find boarded up windows and bullet holes in the walls."

"Yeah, well, it was unsettling to watch it unfold in real time, too."

"At least I had some warning because Mom filled me in on everything after talking to some of her friends and Aunt Cindy."

He snickered. "Small-town living at its best."

"Maybe. But this time I'm grateful for the… gossip-vine, for lack of a better word. Your mom has given Jane's mom daily updates. I know it's meant a lot to Aunt Cindy. Without the updates, she'd be in a constant state of worry, wondering if Jane was alive or not."

"I hope my mother has not disclosed all details. Otherwise, I'm sure Mrs. Mason's mind isn't as much at ease as you think."

Carolina tilted her head. "I'll have to get Jane to fill me in on the missing blanks."

"You've arrived just in time for breakfast. Maybe you girls can catch up after we eat." He turned to walk away.

Carolina put a hand on his arm, halting him. "Thank you for being there for Jane."

He pressed his lips together as the reality that there was nowhere he'd rather be than by Jane's side hit him like a bolt of lightning. With a curt nod, he turned on his heels, got into the ATV and sped up the drive, Carolina close behind.

Dear Lord, my life will never be the same after this. No matter what happens when the authorities capture the man after Jane—whether she agrees to renew our friendship, or she withdraws and blocks me out of her life again—my heart will never be the same. I pray for strength to handle the outcome, come what may.

He parked, grabbed the electronics Jane had asked for and rounded the back of his ATV as Carolina exited her Subaru. "Can I help carry in anything?"

"No. I've got it." She reached into the back seat and withdrew a small suitcase.

He led the way to the side entry, and they entered the kitchen.

"Look who I found," Ridge announced, stepping aside to reveal Carolina.

"Eeek. Carolina! I'm so glad you're home." Jane rushed past him and threw herself into her cousin's arms.

"Me, too. I'm sorry I wasn't there when you needed me," Carolina said.

"I'm glad you weren't here." Jane pulled back. "You could have gotten caught in the crossfire. Where are you staying now that you're home?"

Carolina frowned. "At our house. Where else would I stay?"

Jane gasped. "No. What if the killer attacks you to get to me?"

"Why would he do that? You worry too much." Carolina stepped farther into the room. "I brought you some clothes. Aunt Cindy said you probably need more, since the apartment you were staying in was above the barn that caught on fire. Was it an electrical issue or something?"

"Or something," Ridge's mom spoke up from behind the girls. "We'll have to wait until the official report from the fire chief."

Carolina looked from one of them to the other. "But…?"

"There's evidence to support the theory the man after Jane started the fire," Ridge supplied.

"What evidence?"

"He chained the doors to trap us inside."

"But please don't tell my mom," Jane pleaded. "I don't want her to worry any more than she already is. I'm not asking you to lie to her, but just let her think it was a short in the wiring or something until the report comes in."

"Mmm… Something smells good." Ridge inhaled deeply, trying to change the subject before the tears brimming in Jane's eyes flowed. "I'm starved."

"Well, then come on and have a seat. You, too, Carolina." Mom caught his eye and smiled. Then she guided Carolina through the doorway that led into the dining room.

Jane crossed to the oven. "Go on and grab your seat at the table. I'll be right there."

"I have your electronics." He lifted the bag. "Everything was wet. I dried them the best I could with a towel, but I'm guessing you'll need to use some rubbing alcohol or rice or something to dry all the components."

"Thank you. Just sit them on the counter out of the way for now. I'll deal with it after breakfast. Hopefully, I can save them. But at least I recovered the photos from the crime scene yesterday and upload them to my cloud-based backup storage before this happened."

He placed the bag on the kitchen island, then he took a hesitant step toward her. "Before we join the others, I was wondering if you could tell me what happened in the apartment. I've never known you to be afraid of heights."

"I'm not, usually. I froze. And you had to save me again. That's all it was. Nothing to discuss." She slipped her hands into a pair of oven mitts, opened the oven and pulled out a casserole. Then she brushed past him.

Ridge frowned. He wasn't used to being dismissed. He couldn't force her to share things that she'd rather keep to herself, but he wasn't sure how he would keep her safe if he didn't know her weaknesses.

* * *

Forty-five minutes later, Jane and Carolina sat in the study—Jane's favorite room, with its floor-to-ceiling bookcases and library ladders—where Mrs. Snyder said they could have coffee and catch up while she, Ridge and Wyatt stayed at the dining room table calling friends and neighbors, making arrangements to relocate the horses.

"Tell me all about Hawaii. Did you visit a coffee plantation and hike to a volcano? I can't wait to hear all about it." Jane picked up her coffee mug and took a sip, hoping Carolina would talk about the trip so she could take her mind off her own troubles for a little while.

"I did all of those things and took lots of pictures. I also brought you souvenirs, which are back at the house," Carolina replied. "But I don't want to talk about my trip right now. I'd much rather you fill me in on everything that's happened to you. *And* tell me, how did you end up here, on the Snyder family ranch?"

Jane would have preferred to ignore the question. But she knew Carolina—one year older and more like a sister to her than a cousin— would not allow her to do so. Where to begin? She placed her mug on the small side table and shrugged. "It was timing. Aunt Nikki's murderer cornered me at the school, shooting at me in the stairwell when I tried to escape."

"You're sure it's Aunt Nikki's murderer who's after you?"

"Yes. He made sure I knew it was him." She bit her lip. "The only thing I can't figure out is why he thinks killing me will keep the truth of his identity hidden. There's no way Evan will let this go, especially if he kills me."

"He's not going to kill you," Ridge said, walking into the room. "Sorry. Didn't mean to eavesdrop. But I don't want you thinking like that. I *won't* let him kill you."

"I appreciate your dedication to keeping me alive. You've done a wonderful job of foiling his attempts so far."

"How many attempts are we talking about?" Carolina asked.

"Four." Jane furrowed her brow. "No. Five. On campus, at our house, campus again, the bridge and now the barn." Jane tapped the fingers on her left hand as she counted.

"Five attempts!" Carolina jumped out of her seat and glared at Ridge. "How does he keep getting so close to her?"

"I don't know." He shook his head and sighed. "Evan is working on moving her to another location. And when he does, I'll go with her and keep her safe."

"Another location? Where?" Carolina asked.

"The V—"

"*It's best* if we don't tell you," Ridge interrupted, stopping Jane from replying. "I'm not saying you'd tell anyone where she was, but the fewer people who know, the less of a likelihood the killer will find out."

Annoyance flashed in Carolina's eyes.

"I'm sorry, Carolina, but Ridge is right. If you tell your mom and my mom and they each share with one person they trust…"

Carolina dropped onto the chair she'd recently vacated. "I understand. I don't care what kind of secrets you keep from me. Just stay alive."

"I'll do my best. But what about you? Don't you think you should go stay with your parents until they capture this guy?"

"Why would he come after me? I'm not working with the police trying to capture him."

"I guess." *Lord, I pray she's right.*

"If I see anything suspicious, I'll call Evan and hightail it to my parents' house. Okay?"

Jane smiled. "Thank you."

Ridge cleared his throat. "I came to let you know we found temporary housing for most of the horses."

"That's wonderful! Who is taking them in?"

"Unfortunately, none of our neighbors have

room to house all of them, so they're going to three different locations."

"You said *most of the horses*. Which ones did you not find housing for?"

"The mare and foal. Mom has a couple more calls to make. I'm sure she'll be able to find someone to take them." Ridge frowned. "But I came to tell you that I have to leave the ranch for a couple of hours. The ranches that have agreed to take the horses are in opposite directions. Wyatt is taking four of them to ranches in Colorado Springs and Aurora, and I've got to head to Rocky Ford with the other three. Mom is sure she'll find a place for the mare and colt closer to home. Wyatt will take care of getting them to their temporary home when he returns."

Jane crossed her arms over her stomach. Why was she feeling antsy about Ridge leaving her, even temporarily?

"I'll stick around until you get back," Carolina interjected. "Jane and I still have a lot of catching up to do."

"Good. But make sure Jane gets some rest if you can. I doubt she slept five hours last night." Ridge met Jane's eyes. "Mom, Jake and Fern will be here if you need anything. Please, stay in the house and out of sight. Okay?"

"Stop worrying. I'm sure I'll be fine for a

couple of hours. And I don't need a babysitter. Though I appreciate both of you and your concerns." She gave Carolina a pointed look before turning her attention back to Ridge. "All the attacks have happened at night. He can't move around freely in his ghost mask and black hoodie in the daytime, and I don't think he's going to blow his cover."

"You don't know what he's capable of. He's failed every attempt so far. That alone could make him do something reckless."

"I hear you. And I don't have any plans to leave the safety of the house. But I also don't plan on taking a nap. When I was in college, I survived on a lot less sleep. I have too much to do to take a nap. First, I plan to dry my laptop and check to see if my camera was damaged again. Then, I plan to prod Carolina into telling me all about her trip so I can get my mind off my own troubles."

"Ridge! Where are you?" Wyatt yelled from a different part of the house.

"In the study!" Ridge replied.

The sound of footsteps echoed in the hall, and Wyatt entered the room. "Both trailers are loaded. I need to get on the road since I have farther to go, and multiple stops to make. I wanted to make sure you're leaving right behind me. The Hunters are expecting you before noon."

"I was just letting Jane know what's going on." Ridge met her eyes. "Remember. Stay indoors. Jake has a gun, and he will protect you. I'll be back as quickly as possible."

"I'm fine. Go. Get the horses settled. I'll be here when you return. Hopefully, we'll be able to move to the new location this afternoon."

With a single nod, he turned and rushed out of the room, Wyatt right behind him.

"He's taking his job of protecting you seriously," Carolina observed.

"I wouldn't be sitting here today if he wasn't." A shiver danced along Jane's spine, and she picked up a flower-print throw pillow that rested on the couch beside her, pressing it to her midsection, not desiring Carolina to know how unnerved she was to be separated from Ridge even for a moment. "I really need to get started drying out my electronics. Do you want to stay in here or come with me?"

"I'll come watch."

"Well then, grab your coffee mug and let's go to the kitchen. I should have enough room to work in there as long as Fern doesn't mind."

An hour and a half later, after watching an online DIY video, Jane had opened the casing around the laptop to expose the internal workings, and she'd wiped everything down with rubbing alcohol to the best of her ability. Now it sat on the kitchen island with a small fan blowing on it to dry any remaining moisture.

"That's all I can do. Hopefully, it will work. If not, I guess I'll be shopping for a new laptop. At least I put the camera back into its case before going to bed, so it didn't get wet this time. But I'll take it to the camera repair shop in Pueblo when I get a chance. Make sure none of the internal components are damaged beyond repair." Jane straightened and rolled her shoulders.

Carolina looked at her with an expression of awe on her face. "I've never seen anyone take a laptop apart before. You are pretty incredible."

Jane laughed. "Nope. Just desperate to save thousands of dollars' worth of equipment." She looked around. The kitchen was empty. "Where did everyone go?"

"Mrs. Snyder left twenty minutes ago to take the mare and foal to Mountain View Ranch. You don't remember her coming in and telling us? She said Henry and Oliva Green were attending a charity event in Denver later this afternoon so she had to get the horses to their ranch and settled before they left."

"Hmm. Guess I was too focused on my task.

But what about Jake and Fern, and Molly? They were here when I first started working."

"You really do zone out, don't you?" Carolina teased. "Molly was fussy so Fern took her home, hoping to get her to take a nap in her own bed. Jake is in the old red barn working on the tractor. They all left before Mrs. Snyder did, but she wrote phone numbers on a notepad and left it on the counter over there."

Jane looked where Carolina pointed, spotting the notepad by the coffee maker. "Okay. I doubt we need any of the numbers, but I'm glad she left them. Now, why don't we make ourselves a glass of tea and you can tell me all about your trip? I'm more than ready to hear about something upbeat and not depressing."

Brrring. Brrring. Jane's cell phone rang, and she glanced at the screen. The number was not familiar. Sliding her finger across the screen, she answered the call.

"Hello?"

"Jane, this is Dean Gibson. I hate to bother you, but something urgent has come up. I'm afraid I need you to come to my office immediately."

"I'm sorry. I can't at the moment. I'm—"

"I'm afraid it's not optional," he interrupted her. "There's been a complaint filed against you. If proven true, you will be placed on suspension while a thorough investigation takes place."

It was as if an ice-cold hand had reached into her chest and squeezed her heart. Jane could not lose her job. She loved teaching, and her students and their futures meant everything to her. Whatever the complaint, there was no way she would go down without a fight.

FOURTEEN

"I need to notify Chief Perry that we're almost to campus, so he can have an officer meet us at the visitor parking area in front of the administration building," Jane said, slipping her cell phone out of her pocket. She'd called the head of the campus security before leaving the ranch and told him she'd need an escort while on campus. Being aware of the situation, he'd said he would be happy to oblige.

"I still think you should have talked to Ridge before agreeing to this meeting," Carolina asserted.

"I tried. You know I did. But I kept getting the message, this number is temporarily unavailable. Which means he was out of cell service range. Besides, everything will be fine. The killer does not attack in the daytime, and we'll be back at the ranch long before dark." *Who am I trying to convince, Carolina or myself?*

"Just because he hasn't before, doesn't mean

he won't." Carolina slowed her vehicle and turned into the main entrance to the college. Fire trucks, ambulances and campus security vehicles blocked the road ahead, all with their lights flashing. A multi-vehicle accident appeared to have occurred, blocking traffic in both directions.

"Take a right into the next parking lot. Drive behind the building and take the back exit. It connects to the back entrance of the parking lot of the admin building," Jane instructed as she dialed Chief Perry's direct line.

"Chief Perry," came the gruff greeting, just as she was preparing to hang up on the sixth ring.

"Chief Perry, this is Professor Mason. I've just arrived on campus."

"Oh, sorry, professor. We've had a three-vehicle accident, involving seven students. My officers are all busy assisting the wounded and directing traffic."

Her heart sank, not because she wouldn't have the safety of an officer by her side but because of the injured students. "I understand."

"If you can wait in your vehicle, I should be able to send an officer to assist in fifteen or twenty minutes."

"That won't be necessary. Please, focus on

the students. They are the important ones right now."

Chief Perry disconnected the call. Jane released a slow silent breath, desperate to tamp down the anxiety that threatened to bubble over. She was already on campus. There was no going back. Jane had to meet with Dean Gibson and see what the accusation was and who'd filed it. She could not lose the career she'd worked so hard to build.

"What did he say?" Carolina demanded as she pulled into a visitor parking space and shifted her car into Park.

"The accident we just saw involved three vehicles. There were seven students injured in the crash."

"That's horrible. I'll pray for them to have complete healing."

"Thank you." Jane reached for the door handle.

Carolina put out a hand to halt her. "He's not sending an officer to escort you?"

Jane frowned. "He can't. The injured students take priority."

"Well, then, we'll just have to go back to the ranch. You can call the dean and explain. He can tell you what the charges are over the phone, or he could come to the ranch and do it in person." Carolina shifted into Reverse.

"No, don't," Jane begged, clutching Carolina's arm. "Please. We're already here. I'll just go in quickly, see what the situation is—call my union representative if needed—and come right back out. No detours. And I will make sure I'm never alone."

"You're right. You won't be alone." She shifted the vehicle back into Park, turned off the engine and unfastened her seat belt. "I'm coming with you."

"Dean Gibson won't allow you in the meeting."

"Fine. I'll wait outside his door," Carolina said firmly. "You will not get far from my sight."

Jane recognized the determined look in her cousin's eyes. There was no point arguing with her. *Lord, please, don't let me be leading my cousin into danger.* The instant she'd sent up the silent prayer, it hit her that her concern for Carolina had come too late. The minute they drove off the ranch, she'd put her cousin in a position to be in harm's way. *Lord, forgive me my selfishness.*

"Okay, let's go. But if something happens, I want you to get out of there and get help. Don't be a hero," Jane ordered.

"I'm not leaving you. We go in together, and we come out together. Dead or alive."

"Don't make it sound so ominous. It's the middle of the day. I'm meeting with the dean. That's all."

"You started it with your whole don't-be-a-hero spiel."

Jane hugged her cousin. "I love you. Thank you for keeping it real."

"Ditto. Now, let's go, so we can get this over with and get back to the ranch."

Exiting the vehicle, Jane met Carolina on the sidewalk. As they made their way to the entrance, Jane glanced up. Dean Gibson stood framed in his office window, looking down at them. She could almost feel his displeasure from here. Whatever the complaint against her, he wasn't taking it lightly. Quickening her step, she hurried into the building. The first floor appeared vacant. Only occasional sounds from the student services and financial aid offices indicated anyone else was present.

Normally, Jane would take the stairs since she was too impatient to wait for the older elevator in this building, but the thought of being trapped in a stairwell was unnerving. She led the way to the elevator and pressed the call button, thankful that Dean Gibson's office was on the second floor. In a matter of minutes, they were upstairs, encountering no one else along the way.

Pushing open the door leading to the dean's outer office, Jane was happy to see Mrs. McLean, the dean's personal secretary, at her desk. "Dean Gibson is expecting me. Since it's so hot outside, would it be okay for my cousin to wait for me here?"

"Of course, dear." Mrs. McLean smiled and turned to Carolina. "Would you like anything while you wait? A water or something?"

"No, thank you. I'm fine." Carolina picked up a college brochure off the counter dividing the secretary's space from the waiting area and moved to a leather chair in the corner. "I'll just sit here and stay out of the way."

Dean Gibson's office door flew open. "Professor Mason, I'm glad you could make time for me." He glanced briefly at Carolina and then turned to Mrs. McLean. "You may go to lunch now."

"Yes, sir. I will after I finish typing the letter to the department heads."

"No, now, Mrs. McLean. I have an appointment and will have to leave soon, and you know I don't like leaving the office unattended." He narrowed his eyes. "You can type the letter when you return."

Mrs. McLean's face reddened. She pursed her lips, nodded, withdrew her purse from her desk drawer and marched out of the office. Jane had never seen the woman's composure ruffled before.

"Professor Mason, if you please." Dean Gibson stood aside and motioned for her to go ahead of him into the office. "You realize it's inappropriate for you to bring a friend with you to a meeting. This isn't a social call."

Jane gritted her teeth. She didn't know what had caused the dean to be short-tempered with Mrs. McLean and now her, but she wouldn't allow him to get under her skin. "I'm well aware of the reason for the meeting."

"Don't mind me," Carolina declared, a smile on her face. "Just think of me as a potential student. I'm going to peruse the catalogue and see if there are any classes I might be interested in."

Jane bit back a smile. The thought of Carolina, who held a master's degree in industrial engineering, taking a class at the local community college was amusing. Of course, she could always sign up for one of Jane's photography classes. If Jane still had a job after today.

She walked into the office and turned to face the dean. "You said there was a complaint? I can't imagine what it could be. Apparently, you felt it was serious to call this meeting."

Dean Gibson closed the door and crossed to his desk. "Very serious. Take a seat." He motioned to one of the two leather chairs that were positioned in front of his desk.

Jane sank onto the edge of the chair, not wanting to get too comfortable.

"Summer Fisher emailed me concerning an email you'd sent her with an advance copy of your final exam, complete with answers," Dean Gibson stated matter-of-factly.

"What! No. I never sent her, or any student for that matter, a copy of the test." Why would Summer go to the dean with such a fabricated lie? It didn't make sense.

"Professor Mason—Jane—there's no point denying it. Summer forwarded the email to me." He tapped his computer keyboard, then he turned the screen so she could view it.

On the screen was an email with the subject line Fwd: For You Only, Don't Show Anyone. The sender was Summer Fisher. Dean Gibson smirked at Jane as she leaned over the desk for a closer view.

He scrolled upward, revealing the content of the forwarded message, which identified Jane as the original sender. She narrowed her eyes. The date and time stamp showed the original message had been sent the night of the first attack on Jane, at 11:27 p.m.

"I don't know who sent the email, but it wasn't me. I was at home." She leaned back in the chair and folded her arms across her chest. "And I have a witness."

"You will be allowed to make your case to the board of trustees, but it doesn't look good for you."

"I'm telling you I didn't do it. And I have a solid alibi. One Chief Bradshaw can verify."

"Like I said, you can make your case to the board of trustees." He stood, removed his suit jacket from the back of his chair and put it on, fastening the buttons. "They are waiting on us in the boardroom. I suggest you ask your friend to wait here for your return."

She jumped to her feet. "You didn't say anything about that over the phone."

"Would it have mattered?" He narrowed his eyes. "You don't seem to understand the gravity of the situation."

"I didn't do anything wrong. Someone else sent that email. Not me."

She felt her neck and cheeks warm, tears of frustration burning the backs of her eyes. She closed her eyes, counted to ten and opened them again. As she did, something on the dean's shelf caught her attention. A bookend. In the shape of a king chess piece. Alone. Without a mate. The match to the bookend on Phoebe's bookcase in the photos Jane had restored.

Dear Lord, I've walked straight into the spider's web.

"So… You finally figured it out." Dean Gibson rounded his desk and grabbed her by the elbow. "You're coming with me. And if you don't want anything to happen to Carolina, I suggest you come without a fight."

Her eyes widened. How did he know Carolina's name?

He laughed. "I know more about you than you could ever imagine. I've been watching you, keeping you close, so to speak, ever since you started asking questions about your Aunt Nikki's death. I knew it wasn't casual curiosity on your part and figured one day I'd need to know your habits. And who your family and friends were."

Knock. Knock. The door opened and Mrs. McLean poked her head into the room. "I wanted to let you know I'm back. I decided to just grab a sandwich from the deli and have a working lunch."

While the dean was distracted, Jane pulled her arm free and put distance between her and him.

"That's fine Mrs. McLean. You can keep Jane's cousin company while she and I meet with the trustees," he said, never breaking eye contact with Jane.

"I'm afraid you'll have to reschedule that meeting. I have another appointment." Pushing past Mrs. McLean, Jane darted into the outer waiting area. "Carolina, let's go," she commanded as she speed-walked to the door.

Without a word, Carolina was at her side in two strides. Stepping into the hallway, Jane dared a look over her shoulder. Mrs. McLean was blocking Dean Gibson's path as she seemingly asked him a barrage of questions, but Jane knew he wouldn't be stalled for long.

"Run, as if your life depends on it," she ordered Carolina. "Because it does."

They raced down the hall. Carolina turned toward the elevator, and Jane tugged her arm, guiding her to the stairs. They darted into the stairwell and flew down the stairs.

"He killed… Nikki." Jane panted, fear and adrenaline pushing her to increase her speed.

Carolina matched her steps. They burst out of the stairwell and into the first-floor hall, startling two financial aid office employees who were standing by the vending machines.

"Sorry," Jane and Carolina said in unison, not slowing down until they reached the vehicle.

"Where to? Security office?" Carolina asked as she unlocked the doors.

"No. Police station," Jane replied, jumping into the car and instinctively clicking the door lock.

Carolina started the vehicle and started reversing out of the parking space. *Bang!* Jane screamed. Jogging alongside the vehicle, Dean Gibson peered into the passenger side window and slammed his hand against the roof. *Bang!*

"Stop the car!" he growled.

"Not on your life," Carolina mumbled, put the vehicle into Drive and pressed down on the gas, not slowing even as they jolted over the speed bumps.

Jane pulled out her phone and twisted in her seat, watching as Dean Gibson ran across the lawn toward the gated faculty parking area. He would pursue them until he caught them—of that, she was sure.

FIFTEEN

Brrring! Ridge glanced at the dashboard, expecting to see who was calling. *Ugh.* This wasn't his truck. This was one of the farm trucks. It was old and didn't have the fancy technology newer vehicles have. *Brrring!*

Shifting in his seat, he used his thumb and forefinger to fish his phone out of his back pocket. A quick glance at the screen showed the caller was Jane. Keeping his eyes on the road, he slid his thumb over the screen and put the phone to his ear. "I'm less than a mile away. I'll be there soon."

"Ridge, it's Dean Gibson. He's the killer," Jane said, frantically.

His gut tightened. "What? How did you figure that out?"

"He called. Said there was a complaint. I had to come in. When I did—"

"Wait. Where are you?"

"Carolina and I came to the campus, but—"

"What!" He couldn't believe that she had been reckless and left the safety of the ranch. Only it hadn't been safe last night.

Focus. Jane needs you.

"Okay, so you went to the campus and figured out the killer is Dean Gibson. Where is he? And where are you?"

"We're in Carolina's car, headed to the police station." A sigh sounded across the line. "I'm not sure where Dean Gibson is, but the last time I saw him, he was running for his vehicle so he could follow us."

"Did you call Evan?"

"Carolina is on the phone with him now."

The Rustic Roots Ranch entrance came into view. Ridge slowed, turned into the drive and entered the gate code, thrumming his fingers on the steering wheel impatiently. "Listen. Right now, take a minute and share your location with me. That way, if—" He puffed out a breath, his chest tightening. "If something happens and I can't reach you, I'll still be able to track you."

Clicking sounds came across the line. "Okay, done."

The gate opened, and he accelerated. As soon as he cleared the entrance, he pulled onto the grass at the edge of the drive and parked. "I'll meet you at the police station."

"Thank you," she said, her voice cracking. "I'm sorry I didn't listen to you. I never dreamed the killer was the dean. And I thought I'd be safe in the daylight."

"It's okay, sweetheart. I'm not angry. I just want you to be safe. If anything happens to you—" He swallowed the words *I don't know how I would go on.* It wasn't the right time to tell her what she meant to him. Especially since he was still figuring it all out for himself.

"Don't worry. We'll be careful… No, Carolina. Turn right."

He tucked the phone between his shoulder and his ear, bent over and pressed the button to lower the trailer tongue jack, thankful Wyatt had insisted on paying extra for the feature. "What's happening?"

"We're fine. There was a multi-vehicle accident blocking the main entrance earlier. We're going out the exit near the cafeteria. We'll be at the police station in about ten minutes."

Carolina said something in the background, but he couldn't make out the words.

"What was that?" He released the coupler latch, lifted the trailer off the hitch ball and rolled the trailer backward a few inches, then he lowered it to the ground, ensuring the jack was level.

"Evan has dispatched officers to pick up Dean Gibson."

"Good, but if he made it to his vehicle, he could be anywhere. Evan needs to put out an APB."

"Maybe you should call Evan and tell him how to do *his* job," she said with a nervous laugh.

He could almost picture her holding the phone like a lifeline while chewing on her lower lip the way she'd always done in school when something upset her or she was nervous and didn't know what to do or say. Quickly locating a couple of broken limbs, he placed them behind the trailer tires, chocking the wheels. Wyatt could deal with having the trailer moved back to the barn.

"As long as he keeps you safe, I'll let Evan do his job without interference from me. My only concern is protecting you." Ridge ran to the still-open truck door, hopped into the driver's seat and executed a three-point turn.

"Thank you for caring," Jane whispered in his ear.

His heart squeezed. "Always."

"I'll see you at the police station. Drive carefully," she said, disconnecting the call.

Dear Lord, why did I let Wyatt convince me to leave the ranch? I left her unguarded.

I never should have expected Mom or anyone else to give Jane the same protection that I would have. Please, I beg of You, keep her safe. If anything happens to her, it will be my fault. I failed her.

"I take it Ridge is on his way?"

"Yes. And he had me share my location with him, just in case he needed it." Jane pressed her fingers under her eyes, trying to stem the flow of tears that were leaking from the corners. "I'm sorry that I—"

"Don't you dare apologize," Carolina said forcefully, darting a quick glance in Jane's direction before turning her attention back to the road. "None of this is your fault. Who would have imagined Aunt Nikki's killer was the dean of students at the community college?"

"He wouldn't have been a dean at the time of her death," Jane inserted. "He was a science teacher prior to becoming dean." A former science teacher would know how to rig things so he could pump gas into the ladies' restroom. Why hadn't she thought of that sooner? *Because he was your superior and had never given you a reason to suspect he was an evil person.*

"I hate to point this out, but doesn't it kind

of come down to your word versus his?" Carolina asked.

"What?" Jane frowned.

"I'm asking, what evidence do you have that you could take to a judge that isn't circumstantial?"

"He admitted it to me. Well, basically. And he threatened your life if I didn't go with him."

"Your word versus his."

Anger bubbled up inside Jane. Why was Carolina acting like this? "You saw him. He chased us, banging on your car, demanding we stop."

Carolina slowed to a stop at a red light. "Look, I don't mean to upset you. But he's a prominent member of the community, and nothing you've told me is solid proof."

"Okay, but I do have proof." Jane shifted sideways in her seat. "In the photos of Phoebe's bedroom, there was a bookcase, and there was a lone bookend. It was in the shape of a queen chess piece. On the bookshelf in Dean Gibson's office is the missing bookend, in the shape of a king chess piece."

"Unless you can prove it's the murder weapon—which we know it isn't since they were both strangled—it would be circumstantial."

"Are you sure that you didn't go to law school instead of engineering school?"

Honk. Beep. Toot. Jane looked out the back window. An SUV wove in and out of traffic, erratically. "He found us!"

"Hang on!" Carolina pressed the gas and turned left, causing an oncoming truck to swerve, missing them by inches.

The SUV followed, closing the gap. Dean Gibson was not even trying to disguise his pursuit of them.

"He's getting closer." Jane pulled out her phone.

Before she could dial 911, the SUV rammed into them, knocking the cell out of her hands. It clattered to the floorboard. Jane bent over with her arm outstretched to reach for the phone. There was another jolt as the SUV struck Carolina's car once more, sending their vehicle into a spin.

Jane's head slammed against the dashboard. Pain exploded behind her temples as she straightened in her seat.

"Lord, please, protect us," she prayed aloud.

Carolina's car jumped a curb and sideswiped a row of parked vehicles parked outside a grocery store, coming to a stop near a cart return. Jane scrambled to pick up her phone. Straightening, she glanced over her shoulder. Dean Gibson's SUV was stopped behind them.

"Get out! We've got to run," Jane ordered as she fumbled for the door handle.

The door flew open, and Dean Gibson stood in the opening, disheveled and no longer wearing his suit jacket. He shifted his body slightly to block the view of any onlookers and pulled a gun out of his trousers' pocket. "Don't make any sudden moves, either of you."

"You can't kill us." Jane nodded to the sidewalk where a crowd was gathering. "There are too many witnesses around."

"At this point, I have nothing to lose by taking out any bystander who gets in my way." He leaned in, yet still kept his distance. "If you don't want to see that happen, I suggest you both get out of the vehicle and make your way to mine. Oh, and leave your cell phones behind."

Jane met his eyes. "I'll come with you. Without a fight. But Carolina stays here."

"No. I can't allow that. Unfortunately, she will be a casualty. One you brought into this all by yourself." He grasped Jane's upper arm. The crowd had grown larger. "Change of plans. Carolina, I need you to toss yours and Jane's phones out the window."

Doing as he instructed, Carolina lowered her window, picked up her phone, which rested in the cupholder, and tossed it into the parking lot. Then she accepted Jane's and tossed it as well.

"Jane and I are going to get in the back seat and then, Carolina, I want you to drive us out of town. Understood?"

"Understood," Carolina repeated.

"Is anyone hurt?" someone yelled from within the crowd that had now doubled in size.

"I've called nine-one-one," another person offered.

"There are no injuries. Thank you," Gibson replied. "Please stay back."

He tightened his grip on Jane's arm and hauled her out of her seat. "Tell them you're okay," he said through gritted teeth. "Or I will turn the entire area into a crime scene."

"We're fine. No injuries," Jane declared to everyone within hearing distance, as she allowed Dean Gibson to guide her into the back seat.

"I'm a nurse," a man in his mid-twenties offered, pushing his way through the crowd.

Dean Gibson displayed his gun. "I said stay back!"

The crowd of people gasped. In her peripheral vision, Jane caught movement. A muscular man of medium height was coming from behind. Dean Gibson turned and shot, hitting the man in the upper thigh.

Like a wave, small sections of the crowd surged forward to help the injured man.

"No. Please," Jane begged, tears streaming down her face. Fear of Gibson shooting another innocent soul reverberated through her body. "Get back. Let us leave. Then you can help him."

Carolina straightened in the driver's seat, staring ahead with a blank expression on her face. Dean Gibson nudged Jane with the barrel of the gun. "Open the back door and get in, now."

She did as commanded, and he shoved her into the back seat, following close behind and slamming the door.

"Drive, Carolina, and don't try anything funny unless you want to witness your cousin's death," he growled.

Carolina put the vehicle into Drive and gunned it, pulling into traffic just as a fire truck came into view behind them.

"Step on it!" Dean Gibson ordered.

Jane met Carolina's eyes in the rearview mirror. Dear Lord, Dean Gibson is correct. If I can't find a way to save her, Carolina's death will be my fault. I should have listened to her and waited at the ranch for Ridge's return. Even if it hadn't been a ploy to get me to the campus, no job is worth putting Carolina's life—or mine—in danger.

* * *

Ridge glanced at his watch. Fifteen minutes had passed since Jane's phone call. He thought she would have called by now to let him know she arrived at the police station safely. Maybe she was busy giving her statement. He'd be at the station soon. Ridge should have never left her side. When he saw her, he was going to wrap her in his arms and never let go.

"Lord, why did I reject Jane when she confessed her feelings for me twelve years ago? Sweet, shy, unpretentious, beautiful Jane. Because of my own fears and feelings of inadequacy, I hurt her. It was easier to refuse her than it was to admit that my biggest fear was that if I allowed myself to love her, I would be as bad at marriage as my own parents. I didn't want Jane's feelings for me to turn to hate." Ridge laughed. "She ended up hating me, anyway. Lord, how could I have messed up so badly? There has never been another woman that I've even been remotely interested in. Only Jane. Always Jane."

He heaved a sigh. When Wyatt had married Ashlee, Ridge had thought his brother was making a mistake. He'd even gone to Wyatt and told him all the reasons it was a mistake, starting with them being too young. But Ridge had been wrong. He'd witnessed his brother's marriage grow into something beautiful. The love they'd had for each other had been inspiring. Even today, five years after losing the love of his life and becoming a single parent, Wyatt insisted Ashlee was the only woman he would ever love and he was thankful for the time they'd had together.

"Lord, Wyatt is a wise man. I know he insists he will never love again but, Lord, I pray he does. He and Molly deserve all the happiness in the world."

If Ridge hadn't rejected Jane all those years ago, they could have had a family of their own. And Molly would have had cousins to grow up with. Ridge had always wanted cousins, but neither his mom nor his dad had siblings.

Brrring. His phone rang, jarring him from his wandering thoughts. Police Chief Evan Bradshaw's name flashed on the screen.

Ridge slid a finger across the screen, answering the call. "Evan, I'm so glad you called. I've been—"

"Jane never made it to the police station," Evan interrupted Ridge. "Witnesses saw Allen Gibson run Carolina's vehicle off the road. Wielding a gun and shooting a bystander that tried to intervene, he forced his way into the vehicle and they drove away."

Pressing down on the gas pedal, Ridge increased his speed. "I'm less than five minutes from the police station."

"Come to Cedar Street instead. My officers are questioning witnesses, and I'm asking businesses to pull security footage."

"I'm less than a mile away." Ridge reached a four-way stop and took a right. "When I get there, I can help view security—wait. I almost forgot. I had Jane share her location with me. We can use it to find them."

"The girls' phones are here at the scene. According to witnesses, Gibson made them throw them out the window. Obviously, he was worried about being tracked."

"Did you find a smartwatch?" *Please, Lord, let Jane still be wearing the watch.*

"What?"

"A smartwatch. Did any of your officers find one in the vicinity?"

"Not that I'm aware of," Evan replied. "Is that important?"

"It could be." Ridge approached the area where numerous emergency vehicles sat, with their lights flashing. "I'm pulling up now. Where are you?"

"I'm near the west entrance to the shopping center."

Ridge pulled into the closest parking space, turned off the truck and scanned the area. "I see you."

He disconnected the call and quickly found the location-sharing app and clicked it open. Holding his breath, he waited and prayed. A few seconds later, he saw her location pop up on the screen. "Thank You, Lord!"

Jumping out of the truck, he wove his way around the throng of onlookers and rushed over to Evan. "I know where they are!" he declared breathlessly.

Evan stared at him. "What? How? Where?"

"Like I said, I asked Jane to share her location with me." Ridge turned his phone screen so Evan could see the small blue dot moving east on US Highway 50. "He made the girls dump their phones but obviously he didn't think about checking to see if either of them was wearing a watch with cellular capabilities."

"Sanderson, take over here," Evan yelled to an officer who was taking a statement from a witness a few yards away. The man replied with a thumbs-up. "Okay, let's go."

They ran to Evan's patrol SUV, which he had parked sideways at the entrance to prevent anyone from driving up to the crime scene. Evan activated the siren and put the vehicle into

Drive, beginning to execute a U-turn before Ridge even had his door closed.

"Do you think a siren is a good idea? We don't want him to know we're coming." Ridge clicked his seat belt into place. "And shouldn't we request backup?"

Evan looked over his left shoulder, checking for a clearing, then accelerated as he merged into traffic, other vehicles pulling over to allow him to pass. "I believe I'm very capable and know how to do my job. He's had a fifteen-minute head start. I will use the siren until we get close so I can travel at a faster rate of speed without putting innocent civilians in danger. As for backup, I've already sent out an APB to surrounding law enforcement, giving them a description of Carolina's vehicle, along with its tag number, and making them aware we have two women in a life-or-death situation."

Ridge had done the very thing he'd promised Jane he wouldn't do. He had no business trying to dictate how a rescue would go down. It wasn't his place to overstep the authority of others. "I'm sorry. I shouldn't have questioned you."

A smile crept onto Evan's face, and anger welled inside Ridge.

"I see nothing funny about the situation," he declared.

"Agreed. And I'm not laughing about the situation, or at you. I'm just remembering being in your shoes when Grace was the one being held by a madman."

Ridge puffed out a breath, almost scared of the answer but needing to ask. "What shoes were those?"

"Desperate to save the woman you love so you can tell her you love her and hopefully build a life together."

"You got part of it right. I am in love with Jane. But I messed up the opportunity to build a life with her twelve years ago. So there will be no confessions or dreams of a future together taking place. Just rescuing the woman my soul loves so she can live her best life without me."

"You may not know this, but Grace and I were high school sweethearts. I planned our entire future, saved my money working summer jobs on my neighbor's ranch and bought a ring." Evan spared a quick glance in Ridge's direction before turning his attention back to the road. "The night of our high school graduation, I got down on one knee. She turned me down flat."

High school graduation night.

Why was it, so many times, young adults thought all of life's major decisions had to be made on the momentous occasion of their high school graduation? If Jane had held off on her confession, or if Ridge had pursued the possibility of them dating, albeit long distance with him going into the Navy, could they have found their way to a happy life together? He sighed. Happy endings were a fairy tale, and fairy tales were for children, not grown men who had seen too much death and destruction in their lifetime.

Ridge looked at his phone for an updated location. "They've slowed down," he gasped. "They're at Brush Hollow Reservoir! He's taking them to the same location where he left Nikki's and Phoebe's bodies."

"I don't think he plans to get out of this alive. All signs are pointing more toward a double-murder suicide. His identity has been exposed. There's no escaping his crimes now." Evan accelerated, increasing his speed another seven miles per hour. Then he reached for the car's two-way radio microphone and radioed dispatch, requesting backup. "Hopefully, the girls can get him talking or find another way to distract him long enough for us to reach them."

There wasn't anything else to do but pray. *Lord, please cover Jane and Carolina with Your protection. Let us reach them before it's too late. Evan is right. Jane deserves to know how I feel. If she rejects me, it's no more than I deserve, but I can't let my fear of rejection keep me from telling her how truly amazing she is and how much I love her.*

SIXTEEN

With his gun pressed into her side, as it had been the entire ride, Allen Gibson pulled Jane out of the back seat of the vehicle. *Pop!*

Jane sucked air through her teeth, biting back a yelp as pain radiated through her shoulder. The same excruciating pain she'd experienced in eighth grade when she'd allowed her gymnastics coach to convince her to try out for cheerleading. Some of the popular girls thought it would be fun to put Jane in the flyer position on top of the pyramid. Then, in a perfectly timed execution, those same girls, who were in the base position on the bottom, shifted their weight, causing Jane to tumble from the top, dislocating her shoulder. She'd had surgery, followed by weeks of physical therapy. And she had never tried out to play another sport.

Lord, a dislocated shoulder is preferable to death. I know Ridge is using my location app to track us. Please let him get here before it's too late.

"Carolina, go stand in front of that tree." Gibson used his weapon to point out the tree. "I'll leave it up to you if you want to face the tree or me as I put a bullet into your head. I promise to make it a clean shot so you don't suffer.

"I would have left you behind, but it seemed oddly fitting that there should be two of you, one for Nikki and one for Phoebe." Maniacal laughter erupted from him as he waved his arm in front of Jane, continuing to direct Carolina to the tree he'd chosen. "No, not that one. Over there."

Before she could second-guess her decision, Jane stretched her neck forward and clamped her teeth into his arm. The taste of blood filled her mouth, and she fought to tamp down the instant gag reflex that ensued. Gibson released a gasping yelp and jerked his arm down, the gun firing in the process.

Jane spit out the blood. "Run, Carolina!"

Carolina darted between the trees and disappeared into the weeds and underbrush.

Dean Gibson tightened his grip on Jane's arm with the injured shoulder as he reared his bitten arm upward and smacked her across the face with the side of the gun. Stars exploded behind her eyes, and searing pain splintered outward from her jaw to the top of her head.

"You think a stunt like that is going to stop me?" He twisted Jane's arm behind her back and forced her to a young piñon pine tree.

"Aaahh!" Jane puffed air through her gritted teeth as she focused on pushing the pain to the back of her mind. Frustration-induced tears filled her eyes. She hated to give him the satisfaction of seeing her agony.

He laughed and tucked the gun in his waistband. In one swift move with one hand, he removed his leather belt. He forced her arms around the small tree trunk. Unable to struggle because of the white-hot pain radiating from her right shoulder, she accepted her fate and pressed her eyes closed as he tied her hands together with the belt.

"You just hang out here while I go find your cousin," he sneered.

Oh, Carolina. I hope you ran as far and as fast as you could! Don't let him find you. "Why not...let her go?" Jane panted, her heart thumping against her ribs. "She isn't part of this. I'm the one you're angry with."

"Angry! You think I'm angry with you?" He whirled on her. "I'm not. I'm disappointed in myself for encouraging the board of directors to hire you. For allowing myself to think I owed it to you because your aunt died. I didn't you know. I didn't owe you anything.

"Your aunt is the one responsible for her death, not me. And I owed it to myself to never let anyone know what happened. I vowed to protect my wife and son from what happened years ago, but—" His face twisted in rage. "I should have known having you on campus would be a mistake. That you'd be nosy like your aunt and create problems for me."

Was that a vehicle she heard in the distance? Please let it be Ridge. Don't let it be someone coming to fish—an innocent person, not realizing they were driving into a dangerous situation. Dean Gibson turned his head. *He'd heard it, too. Anger him again to distract him and keep him talking.*

"I don't believe you!" she shrieked. "Aunt Nikki was the sweetest, most gentle soul, who would not *create problems* for anyone...unless *the person* were deserving of the problems." Jane narrowed her eyes. "What did *you do* that made my aunt *create problems* for you?"

"Me? I was minding my own business!" He leaned in close enough that she could smell his lunch. "Nikki was a nosy snoop who wanted to interfere with other people's lives."

Jane maintained eye contact, refusing to flinch, as she fought the urge to gag from the overwhelming breath odor. What could Allen Gibson—a professor at the time—have been up to that would have caused Nikki concern? Her mind flashed on the image of the chess queen bookend in Phoebe's bedroom and the chess king bookend she'd seen in his office. The reality of what had likely taken place hit her in the gut and nausea welled inside her.

Releasing a slow breath, she silently counted to ten as she willed her body to maintain control. Obviously tiring of having the conversation and desperate to find his escapee, Dean Gibson turned away from her and headed in the direction where Carolina was last seen.

"You were a professor. Having an affair with a student was unethical." Jane watched as his steps slowed and he came to a standstill. Bull's-eye. She had hit the target. "I imagine that wasn't the part that bothered Nikki about your affair with her roommate, but rather it was the fact that you were a married man with a small child."

He whirled around, his face bloodred, anger radiating from him like heat from the July sun at midday. "It was none of *her* business. Phoebe and I had something special."

"Then why did you kill her, too?" Movement behind him caught Jane's attention. Carolina hid behind a boulder, listening to every word.

"That was Nikki's fault, not mine. After class, she told Phoebe she had to ask me something about her project for ethics class and not to wait on her. Instead of going home to get ready for our date, Phoebe waited. When Nikki didn't come outside, she came to find her."

"Only Nikki was already dead, wasn't she?" Jane could almost see the scene unfolding before her. "You strangled her in your classroom. With a nylon banding strap, like the ones I've seen around boxes being delivered to Professor Smythe with science experiment supplies inside."

"Yes. She threatened to turn me in to the board of directors and to send evidence of the affair to my wife. Said I was ruining Phoebe's life. That I was the adult authority figure and Phoebe was just a young girl who had turned the entire thing into some kind of romantic fantasy. But that's not true. I loved Phoebe. We would have had a life together. But not if Nikki turned me in and ruined my career and reputation. I couldn't let that happen." He marched toward her. "I've spent the last twenty-three years guarding my secret and building a life that would make Phoebe proud. But you had to insist on poking your nose in where it didn't belong. Now, I've lost everything I've worked for. My life is over, but so is yours."

How could I have been working with Nikki's murderer all these years and not figured this out sooner?

Ridge glared at Evan, who hid behind a Douglas fir about fifteen feet from Ridge's hiding spot behind a boulder. He had assured Evan he wouldn't try to tell him how to do his job, but if the police chief didn't give the signal to move in soon, Ridge might have to go back on his word.

"I don't understand. If you loved her so much, why did you kill Phoebe?" Jane's voice rang out once more. "If I'm going to die anyway, am I not allowed to at least understand why Phoebe had to die, too?"

Gibson stopped a few feet from Jane, pulled his weapon out of his waistband and trained it on her. "She didn't have to die. I never would have killed her."

"Only you did."

Jane's stoic resolve filled Ridge with pride. Gone was the shy, people pleaser who had hidden in plain sight throughout high school. In her place was a strong woman who wasn't afraid to speak up and who wasn't backing down from the bully in front of her. Ridge wanted to rush to her defense but doing so would likely get her killed, since she was between him and Gibson.

"No, Nikki did. She should have known Phoebe wouldn't leave campus without her. They always walked to and from class together. It was their routine. And Phoebe liked routine."

"But why kill her? If she loved you the way you loved her, couldn't you have convinced her to protect your secret? You could have divorced your wife and married Phoebe, and no one would have been any the wiser."

"I told her that, too," Gibson replied, his voice seemingly far away as he recalled what had happened that fateful night. "The instant she looked at Nikki's lifeless body on the floor, I saw her love for me evaporate right before my eyes. She turned to run from me. I grabbed her arm."

Psst. Psst. Ridge looked over at Evan, who motioned he was moving to another location, and Ridge should go the other direction. They'd form a semicircle, closing the gap and positioning themselves so they had better views. Ridge nodded his agreement. He prayed, if Gibson's mind was on the past, he wouldn't notice them in his peripheral vision.

Evan disappeared around the spruce tree. His movements were only detectable by someone who knew to listen for them. Satisfied Evan was in place, Ridge made his move. Dropping to his stomach, he army crawled through the underbrush, making minimal sound. Reaching a thicket of shrubs, he rose to a squatted position and looked around. There was another boulder ten feet away that would put him right behind Gibson. Staying low, he raced to the boulder, sliding in behind it as Gibson turned to look.

Holding his breath, Ridge waited for a gunshot. It never came. He peered around the boulder. Gibson had focused his attention back on Jane.

"It wasn't my fault she fell and hit her head. She was bleeding out all over the carpet. It was more merciful for me to end her suffering," he continued to defend his actions.

Ridge caught Jane's gaze and lifted a finger to his lips. She blinked twice. Something they'd seen in a movie long ago when one of the main characters was in the hospital, unable to speak, and the doctor told them to blink once for *no* and twice for *yes*.

Thank You, Lord, she knows I'm here.

Something touched his arm, and he startled. Thanks to his intensive military training he didn't make a sound. Glancing to his left, he was surprised to find Carolina hiding behind the same boulder.

"Save her," she said so low he could barely hear her.

Ridge leaned in and whispered softly, "I will… Whatever happens, stay out of sight."

He drew back and met her eyes. She nodded and scooted away from him until the shrubs growing around the opposite side of the boulder mostly concealed her. Then she put her back against the rock, pulled her knees to her chest and tucked her head, making herself almost invisible.

"Do you even hear yourself?" Jane bellowed.

Ridge inched around the side of the boulder, his gun at the ready.

"You seriously think you can justify murdering Nikki and Phoebe—someone you claim you loved dearly… Your soulmate?"

"I've had enough of your judgment. I had wanted to find your precious cousin so you could watch me kill her. Knowing your last moments of life were as agonizing as you've made the last week of my life would have brought me great joy." Gibson's lips twisted into a smirk that could only be described as one of the evilest sights Ridge had ever seen, and as a SEAL, he'd witnessed much evil.

Ridge stood. He didn't know what had happened to Evan, but this had to stop now. "Put your gun down, Gibson. It's over."

The dean swung in his direction and fired his weapon, hitting the boulder. Ridge darted behind a tree, thankful the other man wasn't a very good sharpshooter. But even novices could hit their target if they fired often enough.

"I should have known you'd show up, Snyder," Gibson yelled. "Actually, I was surprised when Carolina came with Jane today instead of you."

Ridge peered around the tree. Gibson stood in the opening, his eyes darting left to right as he searched for Ridge. In the background behind the killer, Evan was freeing Jane from the belt that held her hostage.

"Give it up. You know you won't get out of this alive," Ridge yelled.

"I never planned to," came the response.

Evan made the final cut. The belt dropped to the ground with a thud. The sound caught Gibson's attention, and he started to turn.

Quickly tucking his gun into the back of his waistband, Ridge stepped into clear view, his hands high. He could—and would—easily take out the killer, but only if he turned his gun back on Jane. "So, here I am. Talk to me."

"You should have stayed away. Because now, I have to kill you, too." *Bang!* The bullet hit the tree three feet to Ridge's right.

Jane screamed. Evan quickly covered her mouth and whispered in her ear. After one last glance in Ridge's direction, she raced from the tree and disappeared into a thicket several yards away.

Bang! Leaves on a wild azalea to Ridge's left fluttered as the bullet skimmed past. A black-bird squawked and flew out of a nearby bush. Gibson was visibly shaking, sweat staining his shirt. Ridge could easily take him out with one well-placed shot, but he preferred to disarm him and take him alive.

"Come on. Put the gun down and turn yourself in. Don't leave your wife and son to deal with the mess you'll leave behind. Face it like a man."

"Do as he said, Dean. Put the gun down," Evan instructed, his gun trained on the killer.

Gibson swung around, his gun leveled at Evan, who stood close enough that even the most unskilled shooter could make the kill shot. "I see you helped my prisoner escape. Guess I should have known you'd be around here somewhere if the cowboy bodyguard was here." There was a long pause as the two men stood in a standoff. "I'm not going to jail, Chief. You'll have to shoot me."

Reaching behind his back, Ridge pulled his own weapon. While the killer focused on Evan, Ridge, moving with the stealth of a leopard hunting prey, closed some of the gap between himself and Gibson.

"That's not how this is going down, Dean." Evan took a step to his right and Gibson mimicked his move. "I'm taking you in alive. You'll answer for your crimes and serve your time."

Gibson scanned the area, his weapon never wavering. "I'm sure you brought more backup than just the cowboy." He met Ridge's eyes. "If I shoot the cowboy, then you'll have to take me out."

"You don't want to do that," Evan asserted.

"It's the only way," Gibson replied, shifting so his gun pointed at Ridge.

"No!" Jane yelled, stepping into view.

An evil smile crossed the killer's face, and he shifted his focus to Jane. From that point onward, everything happened in warped speed.

"Get down!" Ridge yelled as he dove toward the gunman, tackling him to the ground. The gun flew out of Gibson's hand. Ridge flipped him over onto his stomach and pinned his arms behind his back.

Evan was instantly at his side. "I've got him," he said, grasping Gibson by the upper arm.

Ridge rolled onto the ground, breathing heavily as Evan hauled the killer to his feet and handcuffed him. Ridge pushed to a seated position only to be knocked back to the ground as Jane barreled into him.

"You could have been killed. What were you

thinking?" she demanded, burying her face in his neck.

He wrapped his arms around her waist and held her close. "I could say the same thing. Why would you come out of hiding?"

"I was afraid he was going to shoot you. I don't think I could have handled it if you died."

"Jane!" Carolina ran toward them.

Jane scrambled to her feet and embraced her cousin. "I'm so glad you're alive. I'm sorry I dragged you into this situation."

"It's okay. It's over now." Both girls began to cry.

Ridge stood, noticing that Jane's left arm hung at her side. "You're injured!" he accused, unable to mask the concern in his voice.

"He dislocated my shoulder," she responded. "It's actually kind of numb now."

"That's it. I'm taking you both to the hospital to be checked over. Evan can meet us there to get your statements." Ridge guided them to the clearing where Evan stood talking to two of his officers near a patrol car—Gibson was locked in the back seat.

Carefully guiding Jane to the other side of him, Ridge blocked her view of the killer. He would have to give her a little time to get over the trauma she'd experienced the past five days, but if she would let him, Ridge planned to be her protector for the rest of their lives.

The next morning, Ridge wove his way through the hospital corridor. He had hated leaving Jane last night, but Cindy Mason insisted that he go home to rest while she stayed with her daughter.

The door to Jane's room was slightly ajar. Ridge knocked lightly, not wishing to just barge in on Jane and her mother.

"Come in," Jane called.

Pushing the door open, he was surprised to see Evan sitting in the chair beside Jane's bed. Ridge crossed to the bed and gave Jane a quick hug. "Good morning."

"Good morning." Her rosy cheeks and bright smile indicated she'd had a restful night's sleep.

"Did your mother leave?"

Jane nodded. "You just missed her. She left after Evan arrived. I told her you'd be here soon and you would drive me home after I'm discharged."

His heart swelled. Jane wanted to spend time with him. There might be hope for them, yet. He turned to Evan, not even trying to conceal the joy he felt. "You're out early this morning, Chief."

"Actually, I just stopped by on my way home,"

Evan replied. "I spent the night interrogating Allen Gibson."

"How did it go?"

"He confessed everything." Evan turned to Jane. "Including faking the email from Summer."

She gasped. "What? How was that possible?"

Ridge sat on the edge of the bed—his back against the headboard—shoulder to shoulder with Jane.

"It's not as hard as you'd think. He used an email thread you and he had exchanged a few weeks ago. Went into his inbox, selected forward and then changed the date and text within the old email so it would look like it had originally been sent from you to Summer and then forwarded from Summer to him."

"But I saw it. It was from Summer. If he'd sent it from himself, wouldn't it have shown his email address as the last sender?"

Evan leaned forward. "Did you actually see the return address? Or did he have the email open before you saw it?"

"He had it open, but—" Her eyes widened. "It was scrolled down so I only saw the email message that appeared to be from me to Summer."

"We've obtained a warrant to search his house and his office. His laptop will be taken into evidence, but I have no reason to suspect he's lied about the facts. It would serve him no purpose to do so. He knows he's caught. And he will be spending the rest of his life in jail."

"I can't believe how easily I was fooled." Jane leaned against Ridge's shoulder, and he wrapped his arm around her and pulled her close.

"Don't beat yourself up. You had no reason to doubt what you were being told." Evan shoved to his feet. "I'm going home to see my wife and kids, and to get some sleep. I'll check on you tomorrow."

He smiled, exited the room and pulled the door closed behind him.

Silence blanketed the room. Ridge should move to the now vacant chair, but he did not want to. Holding Jane against his chest after almost losing her was the greatest feeling in the world, one he never wanted to lose. He knew in that moment he had to tell Jane his true feelings. Even if she rejected him, at least she would know he loved her.

Ridge brushed Jane's hair off her face, revealing a bluish-purple bruise on her right cheek. Instinctively, he bent and gently kissed it. "Does it hurt?"

"Not as much as the shoulder." She patted the sling on her left arm. "But thankfully, the pain meds the doctor prescribed are helping."

"That's good."

"Are you okay?" she asked, her eyes searching his. "You've been awfully quiet."

Snap out of it, Snyder. You're coming across as an awkward teenage boy about to ask the girl of his dreams on a date.

He'd faced down aggressors in enemy territory and never once squirmed, but sitting in a hospital bed with the woman who'd confessed her feelings for him twelve years ago, not knowing if she'd accept his love or tell him she was over him, was one of the hardest things he'd done in his thirty years of life. Catching her right hand, he laced his fingers with hers. The seconds stretched to minutes as she waited for his response.

"I'm just relishing in the fact that we're both alive." As soon as the words left his mouth, he regretted them. He pressed his eyes closed. *Justin isn't alive. How could you be so thoughtless?*

Jane put a hand on his shoulder. "It's okay. We *can* celebrate being alive. Justin would expect us to do so."

He opened his eyes and met hers. "I really am sorry that I couldn't save him."

"It wasn't *your* responsibility to save him. I'm sorry I put that on you. Mom said that your mom told her you saved three members of your platoon."

"Yes, but five died."

"Not. Your. Fault." She squeezed his hand. "Now, let's change the subject."

Jane sighed contentedly, resting her head on his shoulder. "This is nice. I've missed you. Our friendship."

"About that." He pulled her hand to his lips and kissed the tips of her fingers. "You are, and will always be, my best friend. I'm sorry I didn't realize how important you were to me when you pulled me aside at the graduation party."

"I never should have done that. It wasn't fair to put you on the spot like that."

"It's also not fair to ask someone to hide their feelings. You were so brave—and stunningly beautiful—that night. I was a scared, naive boy who thought he was being brave, sacrificing a future that he'd secretly dreamed of because you'd be better off without me."

A hint of pink crept up her cheeks. "You secretly dreamed of a future with me in high school?"

"Of course I did. But you have to remember, other than what little time I spent at your house around your parents, I'd never seen what a healthy romantic relationship looked like. I was sure I'd make you hate me inside of a month, so the noble thing to do was to walk away."

"I—"

He touched her lips with one finger, silencing what she'd been about to say. "Please, let me finish."

Wide-eyed, she nodded, and he dropped his hand.

"Witnessing Allen Gibson only thinking of himself, and not his wife and son, hit me hard. I now realize that's what I did on graduation night. There was nothing brave about walking away from the possibility of a future with you. I was a coward. Instead of talking to you and discussing the challenges we might face as a young couple trying to make a long-distance relationship work, I only thought about what I thought was best." He swallowed and took a deep breath. It was now or never. *Please, Lord, let her give me a chance to prove to her how much I love her and show her we can have a future together.*

"I don't want to make the same mistake twice. I don't want to be afraid of what the future may or may not hold. You miss out on a lot of love and beautiful moments when you are afraid to take chances."

She squeezed his hand. "What are you saying?"

"I'm saying that you are so beautiful, selfless and caring. I love you. You are my best friend.

The only woman I can imagine sharing a life with." He puffed out a breath. "But that's jumping the gun. What I'm trying to say is, would you go on a date with me? Give us a chance to explore our feelings for each other?"

"Of course, I'll go on a date with you. I've only waited since ninth grade for you to ask me." Jane laughed, tears streaming down her face. "I love you."

She touched his cheek, and he leaned in, claiming her lips in the sweetest kiss.

Thank You, Lord, for forgiveness and second chances. I promise to cherish Jane and the life we build together.

EPILOGUE

Three months later

A crisp autumn breeze ruffled Jane's hair as she hesitantly opened the door to the hundred-year-old red barn. She hadn't been inside the barn since the night of high school graduation. Ridge had told her they were going on a picnic and to dress warmly. Why would he ask her to meet him here? A thousand imaginary butterflies fluttered inside her stomach. She released a steadying breath and stepped into the building.

Her jaw dropped and she walked forward, mesmerized. The old horse stalls had been removed and large wooden support posts had been installed, leaving the inside of the barn as one large open space. White patio lights had been strung around the posts and along the rafters.

Square hay bales had been arranged like long pews on either side of what had once been the center aisle. At the front of the room, a plaid blanket had been spread on the ground. And several oversized throw pillows were arranged in a semicircle around a bale of hay that held a serving tray laden with iced tea, pulled pork sliders, spinach artichoke rolls, and potato salad.

A wicker picnic basket sat beside the makeshift table, and she lifted the lid. Inside was Fiona's blue ribbon winning peach cobbler cheesecake. Jane's favorite dessert. Ridge had outdone himself.

"You couldn't wait for me? You're already getting into the dessert?"

Jane whirled around and came face-to-face with Ridge. Her breath caught in her chest. He wore dark jeans and a blue flannel shirt, a large bouquet of yellow roses in his arms.

"Hi," she whispered.

"Hi." He kissed her cheek and pressed the roses into her hands. "These are for you."

She pressed her nose into the blossoms and inhaled deeply. "Thank you. They're beautiful."

"What do you think of the changes I've made to the barn?" he asked.

"It looks beautiful. But I'm kind of confused. Why'd you go to so much trouble for a picnic?"

"It's past time that we use this old barn for something besides storage. I thought it would make a great space for entertaining. Can't you picture it decorated for a birthday party? Or a *wedding*? It would be a shame to let something that holds too many important memories to continue to sit and rot."

"Important memories?" She giggled, nervously. "Like the time I fell over the rake and gashed my knee when you, me and Justin played hide-and-seek in here during a rainstorm? Or the time you broke my teenage heart—"

"About that." He reached into his pocket and withdrew a small box. "I thought it was time to replace your last memory of this place with a new, better, memory."

Jane gasped, pressing a shaking hand to her mouth.

"Jane Louisa Mason, I love you with all of my heart. You bring so much joy and adventure into my life. The four years we spent apart, when I couldn't call you or see you or ask your opinion about something, were the most miserable years of my life. I never want to experience anything like that ever again."

Tears of joy leaked out of her eyes. He smiled and brushed them away.

"Your beautiful face is the last thing I want to see at night and the first thing I want to see each morning." Ridge captured her hand and dropped to one knee, with the ring box lid open to reveal a princess cut yellow diamond mounted in a halo setting. "Will you marry me and make me the happiest man that has ever walked the earth?"

"Yes! A thousand times, yes." She sank to her knees and kissed him as the crowd surrounding them exploded in cheers. Pulling back, she looked into his sky-blue eyes. "I love you, now and forever."

* * * * *

*If you liked this story from Rhonda Starnes,
check out her previous
Love Inspired Suspense books:*

Rocky Mountain Revenge
Perilous Wilderness Escape
Tracked Through the Mountain
Abducted at Christmas
Uncovering Colorado Secrets
Cold Case Mountain Murder
Smoky Mountain Escape
In a Killer's Crosshairs
Ambushed in the Night

*Available now from Love Inspired Suspense!
Find more great reads at
www.LoveInspired.com.*

Dear Reader,

I hope you enjoyed meeting Jane and Ridge and seeing their love story unfold as they worked through forgiving themselves and each other for past mistakes.

As Jane learned, it's harder to forgive others if you've allowed pain to create a chasm between you and the Lord. God has given us the ultimate example of forgiveness. We must trust in His love and lean on Him, especially in the difficult times of life.

I would love to hear from you. Please connect with me at www.rhondastarnes.com and follow me on Facebook @RhondaStarnesAuthor.

All my best,
Rhonda Starnes

Get up to 4 Free Books!

We'll send you 2 free books from each series you try
PLUS a free Mystery Gift.

Both the **Love Inspired**® and **Love Inspired**® **Suspense** series feature compelling novels filled with inspirational romance, faith, forgiveness and hope.

YES! Please send me 2 FREE novels from the Love Inspired or Love Inspired Suspense series and my FREE gift (gift is worth about $10 retail). I may cancel anytime by emailing ReaderServiceInfo@Harlequin.com or by calling 1-800-873-8635. If I don't cancel, I will receive 6 brand-new Love Inspired Larger-Print books or Love Inspired Suspense Larger-Print books every month and be billed just $7.19 each in the U.S. or $7.99 each in Canada. That is a savings of 20% off the cover price. It's quite a bargain! Shipping and handling is just 75¢ per book in the U.S. and $1.75 per book in Canada.* I understand that accepting the free books and gift places me under no obligation to buy anything—they are mine to keep for free no matter what I decide.

Choose one:

☐ **Love Inspired Larger-Print**
(122/322 BPA G3CD)

☐ **Love Inspired Suspense Larger-Print**
(107/307 BPA G3CD)

☐ **Or Try Both!**
(122/322 & 107/307 BPA G3CE)

Name (please print)

Address   Apt. #

City   State/Province   Zip/Postal Code

Email: Please check this box ☐ if you would like to receive newsletters and promotional emails from Harlequin Enterprises ULC and its affiliates. You can unsubscribe anytime.

Mail to the **Harlequin Reader Service:**
IN U.S.A.: P.O. Box 1341, Buffalo, NY 14240-8531
IN CANADA: P.O. Box 603, Fort Erie, Ontario L2A 5X3

Want to explore our other series or interested in ebooks? Visit www.ReaderService.com or call 1-800-873-8635.

LIRLIS2603